"[An author] of sensitivity and style."

—*Publishers Weekly*

## SHE'D TAKEN RISKS BEFORE, BUT THEY'D ALWAYS BEEN CALCULATED ONES.

Corey Haraden's case was a tough one. She couldn't begin to weed out the facts.

*What's to weed out? He's charming, successful and dedicated.*

Right. He charms waiters, waitresses and cabbies. He's successful at wheeling and dealing in the office. And he's dedicated to getting me into bed.

*That's because he loves you.*

So he says. But is it a ploy?

*Would he spend so much time and effort on you if it was just a ploy?*

I'm a challenge, that's all.

*Would you rather he do things halfheartedly? Is that the way you want him to love you?*

I don't want him to love me.

*No?*

No.

It was a lie.

"When you care enough to read the very best, the name of Barbara Delinsky should come immediately to mind..."

—*Rave Reviews*

# BARBARA DELINSKY

# CARDINAL RULES

**MIRA BOOKS**

ISBN 1-55166-068-7

CARDINAL RULES

# CARDINAL RULES

# 1

Corey Haraden looped the small monkey's right arm through its left leg and left arm through its right leg, then wrapped its curling tail around its body and tucked in the end. With a single toss in the air, it passed muster. He leaned over, planted his widespread feet firmly, bent his knees and, with both hands curved around the monkey, placed it on the ground. He looked to either side at imaginary teammates on the lush green lawn, called out the play—"eighteen, twenty-three, seven, HUT"—then straightened, gave the monkey a light toss, brought back his leg and connected with a high kick. Sprinting forward, eyes high, he followed the monkey's smooth soar and descent, pivoting to catch it and tuck it neatly into his elbow. A member of the opposing team now, he ran back in the direction from which he'd come, feinting to the left, dodging to the right, freeing himself at every turn from the tacklers who would have taken him down. He ran all the way in for the touchdown, panting, holding the monkey high in victory while invisible crowds roared in silence from nonexistent stands.

"Corey! Good Lord, are you *crazy*?"

Alan Drooker was running across the lawn of his Greenspring Valley home, reaching for the monkey.

"This isn't a football! It's Jocko!" He worked fever-ishly to free the small animal's limbs. "If Scott ever saw you kick him, he'd go insane!"

Corey was instantly contrite. "Gee, Alan, I'm sorry." His voice was sincere enough; it was the danc-ing light in his eyes that gave him away.

Alan, who was checking the monkey over to make sure it was no worse for wear, paused to glare at him. "I'm dead serious. This monkey is *valuable*. It's Scott's prize possession. We had to drive forty min-utes back to a restaurant once when he left it in the john there. Another time, all hell broke loose when its eye fell off. And this is the *second* Jocko. The first melted down in the dryer. Julie made a frantic call to me at work, and I had to go to four stores to find one that looked the same."

Corey did feel guilty then. "Hey, it was just lying there under the tree. I didn't know it meant so much."

"You don't know five-year-old kids," Alan mut-tered, but his alarm had passed and there was a cer-tain wryness in his voice. "This one's a toughie. Wants everything his way or no way at all."

"Sounds familiar," Corey observed, falling into step with Alan as they started toward the house. "Seems to me we both had that problem too."

"Yeah. Except one of us outgrew it."

"You didn't really. You're still that way where work's concerned. It's just here at home that you play second fiddle. I guess having a wife and two kids does that to a man."

Alan looked his share of mischievous with the monkey dangling from his hand. "You can say that again."

"Do you miss the old days?"

Corey and Alan had known each other since college. They'd met as freshmen, had roomed together as sophomores, juniors and seniors. Similar in height, build and good looks, they'd shared a passion for fun, and the old days had certainly been that.

"Sometimes," Alan admitted. "But you give up one thing to gain another. I wanted a wife and kids. It was time."

The blur of a tousle-haired child wearing a T-shirt and shorts sped toward them. "Jocko!"

Alan held out the monkey to his son, who'd no sooner grabbed it when Corey grabbed the boy and hoisted him up, draping him like a towel around his neck. "Gotcha," he growled, delighting in the child's happy squeals.

"Alan!" This time it was Julie, Alan's wife, calling from the open sliding glass doors that led to the living room. "Corinne's here!"

"Corinne?" Corey asked.

"Work. It'll only take a minute." Alan quickened his step. "Wanna keep an eye on Scott?"

Playfully tightening his arms, Corey tipped his head to look into the little boy's face. "He's not going anywhere."

But Scott was. "I want Doritos," he demanded, squirming. "Mommy promised."

Corey swung him down and bent over him without fully releasing his hold. "I thought your mom was busy with Jennifer."

He shook his little head. "Jenny's sleeping. She always does that."

"She's only two. You slept a lot when you were only two."

"I did not," Scott said. His legs were already working, miming the run he'd effect the minute he was free.

"Sure you did. All little kids sleep a lot."

"Not me," he said, then wiggled so vigorously that he'd snaked free before Corey knew what had happened.

In that instant, watching the boy dash full speed toward the house, Corey fully believed him. Of the twenty-four hours Corey had been at the Drookers', Scott hadn't been still for more than six, and then only when exhaustion had taken its toll. He was a bundle of energy, demanding but fun.

Corey could almost understand why Alan had settled down, if settling down was what one would call the three-ring circus that was the Drookers' home. Maybe he'd settle down himself one day—one day way, way, way down the road. Content with that decision, he sauntered in the direction Alan had gone.

"Everything's here," Corinne Fremont said, resting a slim hand on the large manila envelope she'd placed on the desk in Alan's den. "I finished the last of the tables this morning."

Alan was leaning against the desk, his arms crossed over his chest, his mouth drawn into a straight line. "Today's Sunday. Tell me you spent all day Saturday doing the analysis."

She lifted one shoulder in a sheepish shrug. "I spent all day Saturday doing the analysis."

He suspected she'd spent more than the day; all-nighters weren't rare in their line of work, particularly when a client wanted the finished report yesterday. "You didn't have to do that, Cori. You have a right to your own life once in a while."

"I know, but it was my fault the packet wasn't ready on Friday, and we have to make the presentation tomorrow."

"It wasn't your fault. It was Jonathan Alter's fault."

"Jonathan was my responsibility. I should have been on top of him. I guess I assumed that he knew.... Well, he's the computer expert and he came with good recommendations...."

"He came with the recommendation of my brother-in-law, who happens to be Jonathan's third cousin. If anyone's at fault for hiring the kid, it's me."

"He was Phi Beta Kappa at Amherst."

Alan snickered. "For what it's worth. Book learning is one thing, practical application another. A computer is only as good as its programmer, and if he doesn't know what to feed it, we're in trouble. I can't afford to have people like that aboard. I'll have to sit him down—"

"Don't fire him," Corinne pleaded softly. "It was his first mistake."

But Alan was shaking his head. "His first mistake was walking in like he owned the place. His second mistake was being so cocksure of himself that he didn't think to ask questions when he should have. His third mistake was handing you worthless printouts, then turning around and taking off for the weekend."

"Maybe a talk with him will be enough. He'll learn. He's bright, and computer programming is his specialty. All he needs to learn is how to apply our data and where."

"He needs a lot more than that—"

"But he has potential." She pressed on with her argument, unaware of the figure that had silently materialized at the door.

Corey leaned against the jamb and studied the two people as they talked. On the one hand, there was Alan. Wearing a plaid shirt, pleated khaki shorts and deck shoes, he was the image of the successful suburbanite. His dark hair was expertly styled, if casually mussed; his skin bore the bronze of a recent trip to Cape Cod. Tall and fit, he looked even more commanding than he had in their younger days, though those days had never seen the businesslike expression he wore now.

Then there was Corinne. At least, he assumed it was Corinne, since there was no other woman in the room, and if it was a work matter she'd come on, she was business all the way. Even from the rear, which was the only view he had at the moment, he could see that.

She wasn't tall, no more than five-four, he'd guess, and she was slender to the point of being boyish, though he wondered if it was the rest of her that gave that impression. Her dark hair was thick but short, side parted, layered and brushed back in a style many men paid dearly for at the best of salons. She wore a crisp white blouse that was neatly tucked into a pair of immaculately pressed linen pants, whose dark plum shade was echoed in the conservative flats she wore. From where he stood, her only concession to femininity that he could detect was a pair of large, white button earrings clipped to her lobes.

". . . and he's only been with us for a month," she was saying. "It wouldn't be fair to let him go so soon." Her voice was mellow and oddly intriguing.

"He could have blown a big account," Alan pointed out.

"But he didn't. We caught the problem in time. From here on, I'll know to go over the instructions in detail before he sits down at the computer."

"If there were enough hours in the day, you could handle both jobs yourself. But there aren't enough hours, and still you had to do it this time."

"I didn't mind."

Alan's nostrils flared lightly with the breath he took. "You're too soft-hearted, Cori. But if you want to work your weekends away, that's your choice." He raised his eyes to catch Corey pushing off from the doorjamb.

Corinne's head whirled around, and there was a momentary silence. Then Alan cleared his throat and straightened.

"Come on in, Corey. Corinne, meet Corey Haraden. We're just about done," he said to Corey, then to Corinne, "Why don't we discuss this after the meeting tomorrow?" He threw an arm around her shoulder and ushered her from the den. "In the meantime, you can salvage what's left of your weekend."

Corey had the distinct feeling that Alan was hurrying the woman away and wondered why. Not that it took much wondering. Even without the protective arm around her shoulder, Corinne Fremont had a do-not-touch look to her. He noted the sedate paisley tie that had been tucked beneath the back of her collar but emerged into a careful knot just above her breasts, at the precise point where the first button of her blouse lay. As chastity belts went, it made a visible statement. Corey suspected she could take care of herself.

"Wait a sec," he called after the fleeing duo. "What kind of introduction is that? 'Corinne, meet Corey. Say hello and goodbye.' I want to shake hands."

"Corinne has lots to do," Alan advised without slowing his step, but Corey was on their heels, overtaking them in the front foyer.

"Where's your social grace, Alan?" He planted himself directly before them, leaving them no choice but to stop. Then he held out his hand and smiled brilliantly. "I'm pleased to meet you, Corinne."

An expert in social grace, herself, Cori slid her hand into his. "My pleasure, Mr. Haraden."

"Corey, please . . . Cori?"

She dipped her head the slightest bit. It was the most dignified gesture of consent he'd ever seen. "Cori, Corey."

"This could get confusing—"

"Nothing's going to get confusing," Alan interrupted, "because Corinne is on her way." He was elbowing Corey out of the way even as he glanced down at the woman by his side. "I'll see you at nine-thirty. We'll taxi over."

She nodded, then shifted her gaze to Corey when he jockeyed for position in front of the door.

"Hold on. Where's she going now?"

"Home. Aren't you Cori?"

She barely had time to nod again before Corey was speaking.

"Maybe she'd like to stay for the barbecue. What do you say, Cori? We were just going to do up some hot dogs and hamburgs—"

"Cori's been here before and she knows she's more than welcome to stay, but she has other plans. Don't you, Cori?"

"My Lord, Alan, you're *telling* her she has other plans. She may not, and it's a gorgeous Sunday afternoon—"

"That she really should spend with her husband and kids. Isn't that so, Cori?"

But it was a masculine voice that answered. "Oh." Corey took a breath and held out his hand for the second time in as many minutes. "Well, it was nice meeting you, Cori. Have a nice day with your family."

Corinne shook his hand again. She didn't smile. As a matter of fact, Corey realized, she hadn't smiled once. But there was an inkling of amusement in the look she sent Alan.

"See you tomorrow," she told him, then, when Corey had moved aside, crossed the threshold and started down the steps.

"Thanks for the material," Alan added in postscript. "I'll go over it tonight."

"Don't let it interfere with your barbecue," she called without turning, and this time it was her voice that held the inkling of amusement.

She'd barely slid into her car when Alan turned away from the door and rubbed his hands together. "I'm getting hungry. I think I'll light the charcoal."

Corey was frowning at the small white Rabbit as it started slowly down the drive. "She's an interesting woman. Different."

"The hamburg should be defrosted by now." Alan strode across the foyer, heading for the back patio via the kitchen. "Are you any good at making patties?"

With a final glance at the car as it turned onto the street and disappeared, Corey followed his friend. "How long has she been with you?"

"Better still, I like to mix a little stuff in with the hamburg meat. You can score the hot dogs."

"What does she do, exactly?"

"Need any help, Julie?" The last was asked as Alan rounded the doorway of the kitchen.

Julie's voice came from inside the refrigerator. She straightened with an armful of salad makings. "Where's Corinne?"

"Just left."

"And you didn't ask her to stay? Alan, why not? There's more than enough food."

"She had plans."

"What plans?" Julie's eyes narrowed. "She never has plans, at least, not ones any of us would find terribly exciting."

"I'm going to light the grill," said the master of evasion. "I'll be back in a few minutes to doctor up the hamburg." And with that, he left.

Not so Corey. He lounged back against the counter, watching Julie rinse the lettuce. "She must be a hard worker to be at it on a Sunday," he remarked.

"Corinne? She is. And a lovely person, too."

"Seems a little straitlaced." He was thinking of the necktie; it took a meticulous personality to tie a knot that perfect. He didn't have a meticulous personality. His own neckties were almost always askew.

"Very. But isn't she pretty? She always looks so neat." She cast a despairing glance at the spatters of dried baby food on the front of her sundress and chipped at one with a wet thumbnail. "I'm envious. But then, she doesn't have two little imps on her hands."

"No?"

Julie shook her head. "She lives with her grand-mother."

Corey ingested that information, then conjured up a picture of his own grandmother. "Grandmothers can be almost as bad as kids."

"Not this one. She's far from doddering. Mid-sixties, I think."

"And Corinne?"

"Thirty last month. We took her out to dinner on her birthday."

"Mid-sixties. Thirty. Her own parents must have been children when they had her."

Julie shrugged. "Corinne never talks about them. She has a sister who's less than a year younger, though, and married. I don't know why Corinne isn't. She'd make a wonderful wife and mother." She thrust her chin toward a package on the counter. "Congo bars. She baked them for Scott. If you want to taste something good, help yourself. But do it quick, be-fore Scott sees."

Releasing a corner of the neatly wrapped cello-phane, Corey removed a bar, then replaced the wrap-per. He took half of the bar in a single bite and chewed thoughtfully. "You're right. Not bad at all." Pop-ping the second half into his mouth, he brushed his hands over the sink. Only when he'd swallowed the last coconut flake did he speak again. "Alan is pro-tective of Corinne."

"He should be. She's too good to lose."

"He's protective of her even aside from business."

Julie looked up from tearing apart the lettuce to slant him a curious glance. "What makes you say that?"

"He doesn't trust me with her."

Laughing, she returned to her task. "Do you blame him? You're the Cardinal, Corey Haraden. Winging fast and free. You can be sure that when my Jennifer comes of age I won't let her near men like you."

"I'm not that bad."

She raked him from head to toe. The once-over spoke for itself.

Corey dropped his gaze to his worn T-shirt, his frayed cutoffs, then the running shoes that had seen better days. "Okay, so I look pretty messy."

"That wasn't what I meant," she stated dryly. This time, her gaze was more pointed, drifting from broad shoulders down a muscled chest, over deliciously lean hips to a pair of long, tanned legs.

"Oh."

She laughed. "And you look even better when you blush. If I weren't so crazy about my husband, I'd be attacking you myself."

Corey wasn't unaware of his physical appeal. There had been a time when he'd flaunted it for all he'd been worth. But that time had passed. If the truth were told, he was beginning to find the shallowness of it all a little boring. Fulfilling women's sexual fantasies wasn't all it was cracked up to be.

But Corinne Fremont hadn't demanded any kind of fulfillment.

"Tell me more about her."

"Who?"

"Corinne."

"She's not your kind of girl."

Corey realized that Julie wasn't his kind of girl, either, but that didn't stop him from liking her, and it certainly hadn't stopped Alan, whose kind of girl had once been the same as his, from adoring her. "Has Corinne ever been married?"

"She's not your kind of girl."

"Does she date anyone special?"

"She's not your kind of girl."

They were at an impasse. He took a different tack. "How long has she worked for Alan?"

"Five years."

Success, at last. "What does she do?"

"She's an analyst."

"Is she ambitious?" She was certainly serious enough about her work.

"She's capable and dedicated."

"Does she want to move on and up?"

"I've never asked her, but I can't imagine she'd leave Alan. She likes living in Baltimore. The only onward and upward movement for her would be to go with another firm in an administrative capacity. Either that, or start a firm of her own. Come to think of it," Julie mused, tossing a cucumber tail down the disposal, "she'd probably have more free time if she did something like that. She works like a dog."

"Can't have much of a private life."

"She has as much as she wants, I suppose."

"Then she doesn't want much?"

Setting down the knife in mid-tomato, Julie put a hand on her hip and let out a magnanimous sigh. "We're going in circles, I think. Not that it's any of your business, but Corinne has never been married, is neither engaged nor dating someone steadily. She goes out, but with sedate, placid men." She scrunched up her face in a gesture of helplessness. "She really isn't your type, Corey. Why are you asking these questions?"

Corey thought about that. Julie was right; Corinne Fremont wasn't his type. His type was full-figured, she was thin. His type had long hair, hers was short. His type was fun, she was serious. His type was unabashedly feminine, she definitely was not.

He scratched the back of his head, then shrugged. "Beats me."

He was still trying to figure it out late the following morning. Having finished with the business that had originally brought him to Baltimore, he found himself headed for the Inner Harbor, on the fringe of which was the office building housing Alan's market research firm. He'd never visited Alan at work and told himself that was why he'd come. But it was a feeble excuse. The truth was that he wanted another glimpse of Corinne.

A glimpse was all he got when, shortly after noon, Alan and she returned from their meeting. Corey was sitting in the reception area, having endured the come-hither looks thrown his way by the receptionist for a tedious half hour, when the two whisked through. He'd barely risen to his feet when, with a brief wave, Corinne was past him, swallowed by the large doors that led to the firm's inner sanctum.

Alan stopped. "Corey! I didn't expect you here. I thought you had a meeting."

"It wound up an hour ago, so I thought I'd kill a little time. My flight out isn't until later."

Alan cocked his head back toward the elevator. "Come on. Let's get some lunch."

"How about a tour of the office first." He made a cursory sweep of the reception area with its deep mahogany paneling, rich leather furnishings, shining brass fixtures and plush carpeting. "Pretty classy, from what I can see."

He must have sounded innocent enough, or maybe it was that he knew his friend well enough to hit on his weakness, but Alan grinned. "Sure." This time he cocked his head toward the more promising set of doors and set off. "Come on."

Corey followed. He was given blow-by-blow accounts—many of which he'd heard before, but none of which he minded for they were simply a means to an end—of how Alan had taken out loans and double-mortgaged the house to purchase the building three years before, of his fast profits from rental of the floors he didn't need, of his plans for expansion of his own firm in the coming year. He saw Alan's office, an extension in elegance of the reception area. He saw the offices of the three analysts working under Alan and the offices of the field staff with its manager and interviewers. He saw the coding room, the data entry room and the computer room.

But he didn't see Corinne.

"Okay. Where is she?"

They were back in Alan's office. "Who?" he asked, looking about as innocent as a cat with cream on its whiskers.

"You know who."

Alan hesitated for a minute, but he recognized a determined look when he saw one, and a determined look on Corey's face forebode relentlessness. "Corinne?" He shrugged. "I don't know. Maybe she's in the ladies' room. Better still, she's probably gone to lunch."

"Convenient."

"It's lunchtime. The woman has some rights."

"Including deciding who she'll see and who she won't. Come on, Alan. I know she's not married, and I know she's not otherwise committed. What do you have against my talking with her?"

"Corinne's not your kind of girl."

"So Julie kept telling me. Maybe if you let me at her, I'll find out for myself."

"See? Even your words are a threat. Let you at her... I'd be crazy to do that."

"I don't bite."

"I know. You devour."

"Maybe in the old days, but I've mellowed."

Alan's mouth twitched. "Tell me another one."

"She's a mystery lady. Take away the mystery, and I'll probably be bored to tears."

"Not by Corinne. She's one smart cookie."

"Since when have I been attracted to smart cookies?" he drawled in an attempt to show Alan that Corinne was in no danger. It backfired.

"Exactly. So what do you want with her?"

"I'm curious. That's all."

"Curious about what?"

"I don't know," Corey answered more quietly, addressing the question that was beginning to annoy him. "I saw her for all of three minutes, and she struck me as being average. Average looks, average build, average everything. *Too* average. There has to be something beneath all that." Something in those deep brown eyes, he was thinking, but he didn't say it. He couldn't. He'd been called many things in life—a charmer, a devil, a lover, a cad—but never a romantic. Alan would think he'd gone soft. For that matter, maybe he had. "You and Julie like her. Why?"

"I like her because she's smart—quick as a whip and insightful. Julie likes her because she's down to earth, good with the kids and because she's like an alter ego, with the career Julie doesn't have."

"So why shouldn't *I* like her?"

"You should. I suppose you would. I'm just not sure it'd be in Corinne's best interests." Raking a hand through his thick black hair, he circled his desk and sank into the leather executive chair. It was a tactical move, one he obviously hoped would add weight to what he was about to say. "She's special, Corey. She's a private person, prim and proper in many respects. There's never been a special man in her life. She lives quietly, puts in long, hard days—and often nights—at the office, dates carefully and only on occasion, spends her vacations at small inns in no-name towns and never causes trouble. But for all her outer strength, she's vulnerable. I don't want her hurt."

"I won't hurt her. All I want to do is *talk* with her."

"And then what?"

"Then . . . maybe walk away if neither of us is interested in anything more."

"She's probably a virgin."

"Aren't you rushing things a little?"

Alan studied him thoughtfully. "I just thought you ought to know. If she's reached the age of thirty untouched, there must be a reason why." Slowly he shook his head. "I think you should steer clear, my friend."

Corey considered the advice, but what Alan had said only fueled his curiosity. He didn't know why; virgins weren't his style, any more than prudish career women were. He did know, though, that further discussion with Alan would be fruitless—on the subject of Corinne Fremont, at least. So he did the only thing he could. "Warning taken," he said in dismissal, then stood back, scanned the office and sighed. "I'm impressed. You've done well."

Alan was more than willing to let the other matter rest. "Coming from you," he responded with a grin, "that's a compliment. *Now* are you ready for lunch?"

"Sure thing."

Several hours later, after a lunch accompanied by the same easy conversation the two men had always shared, Corey walked Alan back to the office. In the reception area, they shook hands, then laughed and hugged each other.

"Thanks for everything, Alan. It's always great visiting with you and Julie and the kids."

"You'll come again soon?"

"You bet."

Slapping Corey a final few times on the back, Alan grinned, shook his head, then vanished behind the brass-framed doors.

Corey stayed where he was. He smiled when the receptionist looked his way, then, frowning, dug into his trousers pocket. Coins clinked. He withdrew his hand and, still frowning, reached for the inner breast pocket of his blazer. He drew out a card, stared at it, then put it back.

"Forgot something," he told the receptionist as he passed and promptly swung through the doors, ostensibly after Alan. But rather than turning left, in the direction of Alan's office, he turned right. Several doors down, he found what he wanted.

Corinne's office was immaculate. Though Alan hadn't identified it during his tour, Corey had guessed it was hers the moment he'd seen it. The pictures that hung on the walls were straight, the books on the shelves were arranged by height, a caddy on the credenza held an army of identical yellow pencils— sharpened to perfection, he wagered—and the files nearby were arranged in tidy little piles.

Corinne was seated at the desk, a computer print-out spread before her. Her head was bent, propped by the knuckles that grazed her temple. Her free hand lay on the paper, one of those yellow pencils resting comfortably between her fingers. She looked totally engrossed in her work, so much so that another man might have let her be. But Corcy wasn't another man, and he wasn't sure he'd have another chance if he didn't grab the moment.

He spoke softly, in a psssst sort of whisper. "Hi, Cori. Corey, here."

Her head came up, eyes unfocused, but for only a minute. Her knuckles left her face, hand opening to join its mate in utter composure. "Hello, Corey," she said gently. "Still visiting?"

Irrationally he'd hoped for a smile, but he didn't let its absence daunt him. "We just got back from lunch."

"Where did you eat?"

"Phillip's Harborside."

"It's lovely there."

"Too lovely." He patted his stomach. "Too much. Too good."

"Too bad," was her soft refrain, and though he didn't yet get a smile, her eyes twinkled.

"Actually," he said with a sigh, "I could use a little caffeine to keep me awake. Feel like taking a coffee break?"

"Can't do," she said, dropping her eyes to the printout. "I'm behind schedule."

"I can't believe that." He'd put money on the fact that Corinne Fremont was never behind schedule—unless she'd run into a problem like the one that had brought her to Alan's house the afternoon before. "Is the computer doing you in?"

"No, the client is."

"Fussy one?"

"They're all fussy."

"It must be frustrating."

"That's the way it is. You get used to it."

Corey was standing just inside her door, his hands tucked in his trousers pockets. If he didn't know better, he'd have said he felt intimidated by the utter composure she exuded. But, of course, he knew better. "Do you work on a schedule?"

"Always. Unfortunately, the client works on a schedule of his own, and invariably it assumes a miracle or two."

"Are you a miracle worker?" he teased in another bid for a smile, but again he failed. She simply offered that tiny dip of the head he'd seen once before. It could have suggested dignity or modesty, or even shyness. He was intrigued.

"I let *them* think so. It never hurts."

Unable to help himself, he laughed. "Spoken like a true diplomat. So, diplomat, how about that cup of coffee?"

Eyes fixed on his, she shook her head.

"Not even if I throw in a Danish?"

Again she shook her head.

"How about frozen yogurt?"

"I thought you were stuffed."

"I am. I was thinking of you."

"Do you think I'm too thin?"

"I didn't say that," was his reply, but it came a little too quickly and he felt his cheeks grow red. Not even that seemed to affect her.

"I am. But it's a fact of life, like missed deadlines."

"Come on, Cori. Take a little coffee break. Just a little one."

But she shook her head.

"You're sure."

She nodded.

"Not even for a hot fudge sundae?"

Her response to that was the crinkling of her nose, but it came and went so quickly that Corey wasn't sure it hadn't been wishful thinking on his part. He'd wanted something spontaneous; now he wasn't even sure he'd gotten it.

So he made a final stab, using his most endearing and irresistibly boyish tone of voice. "You're *sure*?"

This time, she didn't even bother to nod. Eyes holding his, she slowly lowered her head, then, seconds later, as slowly returned her gaze to the printout. It was, in its way, the most vocal dismissal he'd ever received.

Not one to beat a dead horse, Corey left her office. By the time he'd reached the airport later that afternoon, though, he'd convinced himself that the horse wasn't really dead. He knew it was probably stubbornness on his part or perhaps simply a matter of pride, but women didn't turn him down.

Speeding to the nearest pay phone, he lifted the receiver, stared at the punch buttons, then hung up again. No, a call wouldn't do it. She'd say no again.

He needed to do something that wouldn't allow her to respond, just to think.

Plunging his hand into each and every one of his pockets in turn, he came up empty where notepaper was concerned. So he whipped out his wallet, extracted a rather crumpled dollar bill, straightened it, then patted his pockets for a pen. Seconds later he was striding toward the airline reservation desk and flashing his brightest smile at the female attendant behind the counter. He made a scribbling motion with his hand. "Red, if you have one. Oh, and an envelope? Thanks. You're a lifesaver."

It didn't take him long to jot down a note, seal the bill in the envelope and address it. A quick trip to the gift shop secured a stamp. A jog down the corridor located a mailbox. A flying dash back through the airport saw him safely aboard his plane mere moments before the door was closed and secured.

The following day Corinne received a letter from Delta Airlines. At least, she thought it was a letter until she neatly slit the flap of the envelope and withdrew a dollar bill. On its front, in bold red script, was a succinct message.

"This coupon good for one oversize Hershey's Kiss. Redeemable when you're ready, but only through me. Corey Haraden."

She stared at the note, sighed at the ceiling, then, very neatly, tore the bill in half, then quarters, then eighths, then sixteenths. Gracefully she leaned toward the wastebasket. But at the last minute she paused. Not knowing quite why, she held her hand suspended.

Corey Haraden was a rogue. With his auburn hair, his rugged physique and green eyes that were a trap if she'd ever seen one, he was precisely the kind of man she avoided. Why he was seeking her out, she had no idea.

Nor did she have any idea why she quietly drew back her hand and slipped it into the pocket of her tailored skirt, depositing its contents deep within the lined interior.

More often than not, Corinne missed dinner, and that night was no exception. Her grandmother knew not to expect her unless she called, and fortunately the older woman was more than capable of caring for herself. Still, Cori was quiet as she let herself into the old Victorian house. Elizabeth Strand went to bed at ten on the dot, never before, never after. It was now ten-twenty-seven. Cori didn't want to wake her.

Silently propping her briefcase against the swirling base of the banister, she turned to the venerable maple table that stood beneath a matching mirror in the hall. The day's mail lay in a tidy pile, looking glaringly bland atop the high sheen of the wood.

She lifted the mail and thumbed through, removing one particular piece before heading for the kitchen. She poured herself a large glass of orange juice, replacing the bottle in exactly the same spot in which she'd found it on the refrigerator shelf, took a knife from the nearby drawer and slit open the envelope, then went to the table with her drink in one hand and the letter in the other. She read:

Dear Cori,
I know it was less than a week ago that we talked,

but I need the outlet of writing, so bear with me. I woke up this morning with a splitting headache, and no wonder. Jeffrey was up half the night with the croup—not that I could do anything about it, because Frank says that it's the nanny's job to lose sleep and he won't hear of my getting up—but the noise was awful, so I tossed and turned until Frank told me I was keeping *him* awake. You'd think the man would be concerned about his own son, but he has this incredible ability to dole out authority and then turn his back on the rest of the world and focus his concern on himself.

It works with his business. Heaven knows he's successful enough, and I suppose I should be grateful. I don't have to worry about a thing—but that's the problem. I feel useless. When Frank isn't at the office, he's in his den reading the paper, and when we go out there always has to be a purpose to it. Either we're entertaining a potential client, or repaying a dinner invitation, or getting one up on another. I can't remember the last time we did anything for fun.

Fun. An involuntary shiver rippled through Cori as, slowly and sadly, she turned the page and read on.

I know what you're thinking. Yes, I should thank my lucky stars that I have a responsible husband. No, I shouldn't be pining for fun, because fun means carefree and carefree is what Mom and Dad are and look where it's gotten them—or rather, us. The irony of it is that they were barely out of their teens when they had us, and they were thrilled to take off and leave us with Gram, while I would like nothing better than to take care of my own son and my own house and my own food shopping and my own wardrobe. Frank won't let me.

Maybe it's his age. Forty-five isn't that old, but he's an old forty-five. He's stubborn and set in his ways and has the pride of a dozen people combined. No wife of *his* is going to work around the house, he says—as though the milkman will see and tell his friends and there will be a horrible scandal because Frank Shilton's wife was caught loading the dishwasher.

I'm bored. There are times when I envy you your career—ever think you'd hear me say that? There are also times when I envy Mom and Dad their flakiness. You've heard me say *that* a million times, and you've chided me as often, but there is something to be said for being free. I'm not. I feel caged. Granted, the cage is gilded, but what good is it if the bird inside is stifling?

With a shaky hand Cori set aside the second sheet of paper. She glanced at the phone, then the clock and, wincing, picked up the third and last page of the letter.

No, don't call me. If I know you, it'll be late when you finally get home and read this. You'll be sitting in the kitchen with your orange juice, and Gram will be upstairs in bed. For that matter, so will Frank. And besides, I'm sure the crisis will have passed and I'll be feeling better. It's just that sometimes I get so down. I wish you could understand that, but I doubt you've had a down day in your life. You're so even-tempered. I envy you that, too.

You can go on up to bed now. I'll be thinking of you—hanging your clothes in the closet, reaching for the towel on the right side of the bar after your shower, turning down the left side of the bed and checking, then double-checking the alarm clock on the nightstand. Fond memories, really. You always were the stabilizing force in my life. I guess you were preparing me for what I have now, huh?

Thanks for the ear, Cori. You may be a stick-in-the mud at times, but you're a good sister.

It was signed, "Love, Roxanne." And there was a P.S. "It's a good thing Gram wouldn't dream of opening anyone else's mail. If she reads this letter, she'll think she's truly failed in her mission."

Cori sat for a long time with the last page of the letter in her hand. *Gram's mission, or mine?* she wondered, feeling strangely unsettled. Though Roxanne was barely a year younger than she, Cori had always been the older sister in every sense of the word. She'd been the one who'd kept after Roxanne to do her homework, who'd yelled at her when she'd skipped a class, who'd looked over her shoulder while she was filling out applications for college. She'd been the one who'd set curfews and had waited up in agony when they were missed. And she'd been the one who'd been heartily in favor of Roxanne's marriage to Frank.

*She's approaching thirty. That's what this is all about.*

I turned thirty without any problem.

*You turned thirty when you were eighteen.*
Well, it was painless.
*Roxanne isn't you. She's always had a wild streak.*
I curbed it.
*You thought.*
Cori knew that she could argue with herself forever, but the fact remained that Roxanne was an adult. Cori had done her best, as had their grandmother. It was up to Roxanne, now, to come to terms with her life.

Wishing it was as simple as it sounded, Cori carefully folded the letter and slid it back in its envelope. She drank the last of her juice, rinsed the glass and placed it in the dishwasher, then wiped the sink until it was as shiny as ever. Then she turned off the lights and tiptoed upstairs, knowing precisely which steps creaked where and how to avoid them.

She was tired, but that didn't stop her from hanging her clothes neatly in the closet. Rather than a shower, she took a long bath, but still she reached for the towel on the right when she was done. Padding softly back to the bedroom, she turned down the left side of the bed, checked and double-checked the alarm clock on the night stand, then sighed as she slipped between the sheets.

For the first time in her life, she thought they felt too starchy.

## 2

Corey knew he was disorganized. His secretary told him so at least twice a day when she had to unearth one critical document or another from the mound of papers on his desk. And if it wasn't his secretary, it was his housekeeper, who threatened to quit each time she found the ketchup in the freezer between the TV dinners and the frozen pizza, or the ice cream in the cabinet melting against the Rice Krispies. Corey argued that life was too short for anyone to be worried about trivialities, but the fact was that too often his mind raced ahead of the task at hand before that task was quite finished.

In the days that followed his trip to Baltimore, his mind was indeed racing ahead. He pictured a follow-up trip, during which he would invite Corinne Fremont to dinner and extract a smile. He then visualized another trip, during which he would take her on a picnic and make her laugh. On their third date he'd put bright color on her cheeks; on their fourth he'd see that her clothes were rumpled a bit. And on their fifth he'd very carefully peel off those clothes and discover that there was a woman of passion beneath.

Or so the fantasy went. He wondered when he'd become prone to fantasizing, then realized that it was simply an erotic extension of imagining. And he'd always been one to imagine.

When he'd been a kid, he'd imagined owning a building, so he'd bought one soon after he'd received his graduate degree in business. The building had been in a not so super area of Philadelphia, but that hadn't mattered, because he'd gutted it, rebuilt it and—just when the rest of the neighborhood was catching on to the idea of gentrification—sold it for five times what he'd paid.

But he'd barely reached that point of resale when he'd imagined building something from scratch. The ink hadn't been dry on the final deed of sale when he'd turned his profit around and invested it in a piece of open land, this one in a suburban area. There he'd proceeded to build an office complex.

Before he'd completed the complex, he'd imagined creating a shopping mall nearby. So he'd gathered a group of investors, put together a package and gone on to construct a thirty-five-store mall. Neiman Marcus had no sooner signed on as one of the anchor stores when he'd imagined buying a hotel, which he'd proceeded to do once, twice, then three times.

He'd never set his powers of imagination to work on a woman before, though. From the time he'd been sixteen, females had been his for the taking. Corinne Fremont wasn't his, and she wasn't for the taking, which was perhaps why he wanted her. No, he corrected himself, it wasn't that he *wanted* her, not in the physical sense of the word.... Though if his fantasies approached reality, that might be true in time. More immediately, he wanted to get to know her.

His initial reaction to her was apt. She was different. And being different, she'd necessitate a different approach on his part. She was a guarded woman. He sensed he'd have to play by her rules at the start.

Therefore he waited three weeks before he made an attempt to contact her. He was giving her time. He wasn't rushing her. He'd let her read and reread the note he'd sent and hope that her mouth was beginning to water.

It was a Tuesday afternoon, and Corinne was at work. When the phone on her desk bleeped, she lifted it distractedly.

"Yes?"

"Cori? This is Corey Haraden."

Disoriented, she frowned at the phone. She'd been making a preliminary outline for a newly contracted survey and had been preoccupied enough not to notice that the bleep she'd responded to hadn't come from the intraoffice line. Laying down her pencil, she straightened in her seat.

"Hello, Corey. How are you?"

"Fine, thanks. And you?"

"Very well." She thought of an oversize Hershey's Kiss, then thought again. "If you're looking for Alan, he's not here. Did you try his office?"

"I wasn't looking for Alan. I was looking for you. Listen, I know you're probably up to your ears in work, but I'm in Rochester and my plane has a two-hour layover in Baltimore before it heads on to Atlanta. How about meeting me for dinner?"

That didn't take any thought at all. "I'm sorry, Corey, but I can't."

"Are you still behind schedule?"

"That depends on whose schedule you're talking about, but I think we've already discussed this."

"We could discuss it again. I won't mind."

The irony of it was that he sounded so kind and sincere that if Corinne had never met him, she might have considered accepting his invitation. But she had met him. She'd seen him. He was trouble. "I'd mind. It'd be pretty boring."

"Boring? No way! I've been called impulsive and irrepressible, even glib, but never boring."

Which was one of the reasons she didn't want to see him. "I'm sure," she said dryly.

"You can't work all the time, and you have to eat dinner."

"It's not that, Corey. I have other plans."

"Oh." He sighed. "Another family night. Husband and kids."

His tone suggested he was teasing. She went along with it. "Right. They get pretty impatient with me sometimes."

"I can understand that," was his own wry retort. Every instinct told him to press, but, then, his instincts had been honed on women other than Corinne. "Well, maybe another time?"

"Maybe." It was as noncommittal as she could get without being rude.

"Okay. I guess I'll just have to walk around by myself for two hours then."

Corinne's heart didn't bleed easily, nor was she about to feel guilty. "You'll find company. The flight attendants will have two hours to spare, also."

"I do not pick up flight attendants," he stated, then his tone mellowed to one of resignation. "Besides, half of them are male nowadays."

"As rightly they should be."

"Come on, it's not *that* dirty a job. Stewardesses may be glorified waitresses, but they have a good time for themselves."

"Exactly. Isn't it nice now that men can share the good time?"

Corey laughed, partly at what she'd said, partly at the way she'd said it. He could have sworn she was smiling. "Touché," he said gently, then turned his head when an amplified voice sounded through the airport. "Uh-oh. They're calling my flight. I don't think they'll want to hold it for me again."

"Again?"

"I have a habit of being late. The airlines know me by now."

"Do you fly a lot?"

"A lot," he said with feeling.

"What is it you do, exactly?"

"Damn it, there they go again. Final call for boarding. I really have to run, Cori. I'll talk with you later, okay?"

Corinne didn't want to touch that question. As it was, she was feeling vaguely disappointed and she didn't understand why. "Have a safe trip."

"Sure thing. Take care." Replacing the receiver, he dashed from the booth, but there was a smug smile on his face as he sprinted toward the plane. *What is it you do, exactly?* He couldn't have timed the end of their conversation better. Let her wonder. And think. She might not be actually drooling, but she was curious. It was a start.

Corinne was definitely not curious, or so she told herself. But quite unbidden, Corey Haraden's face kept popping up in her mind, and at the strangest times, such as when Tom O'Neill was driving her home after a pleasant evening at the theater Thursday night, and when she was extolling the virtues of Frank Shilton to her sister on Sunday, and when she and Alan spent three hours in conference Tuesday morning with a particularly stubborn client.

It occurred to her that Alan could well tell her more about Corey, but she was damned if she'd ask. For one thing, she knew how close the two men were. For another, she knew that Alan hadn't wanted her anywhere near Corey. She didn't want Alan to know Corey had called her, lest it put a wedge between the men. Nor did she want Alan to think that she was interested in Corey. Because she wasn't.

He was the antithesis of the type of man she dated. Tom O'Neill was an accountant. Of medium height and build, he was pleasant to look at and to be with. He was polite and reserved, and he shared her fascination with numbers. He was also as uninterested in a deep relationship as she was, which meant they could enjoy a dinner together on occasion, or a show or a movie, with no strings attached. They rarely saw each other more than twice a month and were simply and platonically friends.

From time to time she dated Richard Bates. Twice married and twice divorced, Richard had sworn off permanent relationships and was simply out for a little intellectual stimulation. Cori could certainly provide that, because she was a listener and a thinker and she expressed herself well. He was an economics professor at Johns Hopkins, and she found the discussions they had to be informative and thought provoking.

There were other men in her life, men she saw once every few months, and there had been men in the past. They had varied backgrounds and occupations. Cori thought of them almost as accessories to be worn for a little flavor now and again. Like accessories, they never overshadowed her basic ensemble, and like accessories, they were easily discarded.

It didn't take great intuitiveness to know that Corey Haraden would refuse to be an accessory. Nor did it take a sharp eye to see that he'd clash with her style. He was titian to her pale pink, turquoise to her baby blue, lime green to her olive.

The men in her life were either gray or tan, and she was more than happy to keep it that way.

As the days passed, she came to regard her thoughts of Corey as nothing more than momentary distractions, like the horror movie she'd seen on television and then relived in brief flashes for a time after. There were too many things to truly occupy her—her work, her concern for Roxanne, her plans for the weekend or her next vacation or an outing with her grandmother—to waste thought on Corey Haraden. She assumed that, as the horror movie had done, memory of him would eventually fade into oblivion.

She hadn't counted on the fact that he would appear, in the flesh, at the door of her office on a Friday afternoon in early May. Nearly a month had passed since she'd heard from him last, and she'd succeeded in erasing him from her mind, only to have a fresh imprint made now.

He was a striking figure, but she'd known that from the first. Whereas at Alan's house he'd been the rugged jock, and the next day at the office he'd been the spiffy man-about-town, today he was an executive through and through. He wore a tailor-made suit of summer tweed, a white shirt and a striped tie—perfectly, if painstakingly knotted—that picked up the blue and gray of his jacket and trousers, and leather shoes that couldn't have been more Italian if they'd been tricolored, green, white and red. His auburn hair was carefully styled, if on the long side, and his tan was deeper than it had been before.

In the three times she'd seen him, though, one thing remained constant. His eyes. Green and riveting. Sharp and probing. Soft and beckoning.

Corinne didn't want to be beckoned. She didn't want to be probed or riveted. In fact she wanted him to vanish in a puff of smoke, never to be seen or heard from again.

There was no puff of smoke, though, and when she closed her eyes, then opened them a second later, he was still there. The worst of it was that her heart was thudding. She didn't like that one bit.

"Still working, I see," he teased, foregoing the preliminaries as he rested an arm high on the doorjamb. A slim gold watch peeked from the cuff of his shirt, adding even greater elegance to his attire.

"That's right," she said. But she quickly gathered together the papers she'd been reading. "As a matter of fact—" she neatened the pile with several effective whacks on the desk "—I'm on my way out."

"Where to?"

She reached for a file from the credenza and inserted the papers. "A meeting."

"Here?"

"Uh-huh. My coders are waiting for instructions." The fact was the coders were expecting her later in the day. At the moment, she didn't care. If they were ready, fine; if not, fine, too. Corey Haraden didn't have to know what went on behind the closed doors of the coding room.

"Can I come along?"

She hugged the file to her chest and pulled several evenly sharpened pencils from the caddy. "Afraid not."

"How come?" he asked, straightening as she approached.

"Confidentiality. Our clients are almost as fussy about it as they are about urgency."

"I won't breathe a word to anyone about anything."

Coming even with him, she tipped up her head, then had to call on her deepest reserves to remain composed. He was tall and broad shouldered, imposing, to say the least. Apart from that, there was something about the tiny laugh lines at the corners of his eyes and the hair that fell rakishly across his brow and the faint shadow underlining the smoothness of his jaw that did funny things to her stomach.

But composed she remained, only the uncharacteristic edge to her voice revealing the fact that she felt anything at all. "Why would you be interested in my meeting?"

"I'd like to see what you do."

"Why?"

"Because you look to be very efficient. Maybe I'll learn something."

"Are you thinking of becoming an analyst?"

The corner of his mouth twitched. "Not quite."

"Then what could I possibly have to teach you?"

"Management techniques are universal. I'd enjoy seeing how you handle your coders."

Given what she felt to be a plausible excuse, she let her eyes score his length. "You look more like an executive than a manager."

"I am, but every executive is a manager of sorts."

"What do you execute?" she asked, not at all dissatisfied with the pun.

Corey was aware of the play on words, just as he was aware that Corinne was more of an intellectual match for him than he'd met in a long while. He could have offered her something suggestive in reply—*I execute available young women; does that scare you?*—but somehow he didn't think she'd appreciate that, so instead he answered forthrightly, if briefly.

"I'm in real estate. Hotels, mostly. And I'm afraid I'm not the best of managers. I usually leave that chore to others. So, what do you say? Can I go to your meeting?"

"Hotels. I'm impressed."

"Can I go?"

"How many hotels?"

"Three. How about that meeting?"

"Do you have one here in Baltimore?"

"A meeting? No, not on this visit."

"A hotel."

"I'm working on it." He sighed. "Why do you keep avoiding the question?"

Corinne slid him a reproachful look. "Because I've already answered it twice." She went through the door and started down the hall.

Corey fell into step beside her. "Do I annoy you?"

"Yes."

"Why?"

"Because you're like a horse sniffing for sugar, and I'm out of cubes."

Corey scratched the back of his head. "A horse. That's a new one." His hand fell away. "But I don't want sugar. All I want is a little of your time."

"For what?"

"To *talk*. Just to *talk*."

"Shhhh." She glanced toward one of the offices they passed and spoke in a half whisper. "Unless you want to add embarrass to annoy, keep your voice down."

Impulsiveness was as characteristic of Corey as his red-brown hair. He'd done his best to curb it where Corinne was concerned, but it flared now, and he had the advantage of surprise. Clamping his long fingers around her arms, he backed her against the nearest wall, then flattened his forearms on the grass cloth on either side of her head. His slanting body was the door of her prison. She was penned in, exactly as he wanted her.

He spoke softly, close by her ear. "I'll add embarrass and any number of other verbs to the list if you don't give me a little satisfaction, Corinne. Don't ask me why it matters, because I can't figure it out myself, but I do know that I need to talk with you."

She took a breath and opened her mouth to speak, then closed it when, in the same low, almost intimate tone, he went on.

"'About what?' you were going to say. See? I know you already. Smart little retorts from a smart little mouth. But I want more, and I won't give up until I get it. So. What'll it be? A scene here in the hall or a nice, calm chat when you're done with your meeting?"

"I thought you wanted to go to my meeting?" she asked, slightly peeved by the weakness in her voice.

Being a breath away from Corey Haraden, feeling his warmth, smelling the scent that was natural and clean and could never have been bottled in a million years— those things did something to her. She didn't like it, but there it was.

"I lied," he said smoothly.

"Then we're even because I don't have a meeting." She tried to slip under his arm but he simply lowered it, forcing her even more rigidly against the wall. The arm holding file and pencils was the only thing between them.

"We'll talk now, then."

Her hair brushed against the grass cloth as she shook her head, and the eyes she raised to his held equal parts of fear and defiance. "I have to work. My meeting with the coders is later. If I don't finish going through these papers, that meeting will be a waste of time for them, as well as for me."

"Then later. We'll talk later."

"I can't. The meeting will run till the end of the day, and I have a date for dinner."

"Let's not joke about the husband and kids."

"Okay. It's with my grandmother."

Corey leaned even closer. His cheek grazed hers, his mouth touched her ear. Today she was wearing black button earrings to match her skirt. The enamel felt cool against his skin. "Try again."

"It is," she insisted in a shaky breath. She was pressed stiffly against the wall, but still she felt flimsy. Without realizing what she was doing, she closed her eyes and moved her cheek just a bit against his. The friction was electric. Her eyes flew open and she swallowed hard. "I promised my grandmother that I'd take her out."

"Have a drink with me, *then* take her out."

"I can't. She has to eat at six on the dot. Corey, please move. Anyone could walk out here—"

"Why does she have to eat at six? Is she sick?"

"She *likes* to eat at six. Please, Corey..."

"Take me with you."

"I can't. She'd be appalled."

"I'd charm her."

"You'd terrify her."

"Like I terrify you?"

"You don't terrify me. Corey..." she warned, but he wasn't through.

"I'd like to meet your grandmother."

"No, you wouldn't. She's starchy."

"So are you, but there's something to be said for starch. It takes a little effort to wrinkle, but the challenge is worth it."

"Is that what I am? A challenge?"

"Yes."

"And that's why you're being such a pest?"

"Yes."

"If I agree to talk with you, will you go away?"

"I'll decide that after we talk."

"Corey..."

"Cori?"

"That's not fair." Unaware that her free palm bore the imprint of the grass cloth, she squeezed that hand between their bodies and pushed, only to find that his chest was as immovable as the wall. "Let me go."

His voice grew even softer. "I like it when you touch me. I didn't know if I would, but I do."

Her hand went limp, and this time when she closed her eyes, it was in a bid for strength. "Please," she whispered.

"Will you talk with me?"

"Yes."

"When?"

"I . . . I don't know."

"When?"

"Tomorrow."

"When tomorrow?"

"Uh . . . I have aerobics at ten. We can meet for coffee at eleven, but I'll have to be home by twelve."

"Why twelve?"

"I have to clean up. I'm baby-sitting at one."

*"Baby-sitting?"*

"Pleeeeease, Corey."

He lowered his voice again, but he wasn't about to free her until he had a firm commitment. "Okay. I'll ask you about that one tomorrow. Where should I be at eleven?"

She mumbled the address of a small coffee shop not far from the church where the aerobics classes were held.

"Better still, where's your class? I don't trust you. You'll stand me up."

She gave a broken laugh. "And have you tracking me down like a bloodhound? No way. I want this over and done."

"Where's the class?"

She gritted her teeth and said nothing until he slid the lower part of his body against her, at which point she quickly blurted out the name and address of the church.

"Thank you," he said, and slowly levered himself away. He took a step back, then smiled at her. "There. That wasn't so bad, was it?"

Corinne was incredulous, and the heightened pitch of her voice showed it. "You're a bully."

"Sometimes it takes a little bullying to get what I want. If you'd agreed to see me at the start, I wouldn't have had to resort to bullying. You ought to keep that in mind, Cori. Sugar works over vinegar any day." He frowned for an instant, recalling her comment about the horse, then he wiped the frown clean and grinned. "I'll see you at the church at eleven tomorrow, then. Ciao." Turning on his heel, he was striding down the hall before she could think of a suitable retort. All she could do now was relax her stranglehold on the file and pencils, straighten her skirt, tip up her chin and return to her office as though nothing had ever happened.

*Nothing did happen, silly.*

Nothing? You call harassment nothing?

*He was right, you know. You gave him no other choice.*

He could have accepted a simple no.

*He didn't want to. So he's stubborn, so what?*

He's arrogant as hell, and I don't like him.

*Is that why you were trembling enough to wrinkle your stockings?*

I was trembling because I was in a situation that I couldn't control.

*You can't have it your own way all the time.*

Oh, no?

When Corinne emerged from her aerobics class the next morning, she looked like a reject from boot camp. At least, that was what she thought, and it was what she'd intended. Her hair was damp and clung to the nape of her neck in spikes, her face was bare of makeup. She was wearing a sweat suit that had once been the color of mustard but, thanks to too many washings, now resembled the mustard itself—lumpy and shapeless. Not to mention that she was sweaty, probably smelly, and very definitely unappealing. That was exactly what she'd planned.

Unfortunately, Corey's attitude toward a reject from boot camp was quite different from hers. He gaped. "I don't believe it!" Then he grinned. "You look terrific!"

For an instant she stared at him in disbelief. Then her heart dropped. "Sure." She should have known it. The first time she'd seen him he'd looked pretty grungy himself. No doubt he preferred the battered look.

What she didn't realize was that rather than looking battered, in Corey's eyes she looked human. And young. And healthy. Her cheeks had a natural flush; her hair was lush in disarray. True, the sweat suit was shapeless, but he had no trouble imagining the leotard she wore beneath. His only regret was that the door to the room in which her class was held didn't have a window. He would have liked to have seen her in action, wearing that leotard, moving to the gripping beat of the rock music he'd heard.

"How'd it go?" he asked, looping his arm through hers.

She whipped her elbow free. "Don't touch me! I'm awful!"

"You're not awful." This time when he drew her arm through his, he locked their fingers together. She wasn't getting away so quickly a second time. "Was it fun?"

"It's always fun."

"You do it every Saturday?"

"Yes."

"Are you angry at me?"

"Yes." In truth, she was angry with herself. She had a newer sweat suit and sneakers, and she could have easily washed up at the church, as she often did when she had errands to run right after class. She'd been hoping to keep Corey at a distance by looking atrocious, but it hadn't worked. Deprived of satisfaction, she simply felt ugly. She was angry about that. And, yes, she was angry at Corey because he hadn't been fazed and because, even in casual jeans and a polo shirt, he looked good and because she shouldn't feel badly about feeling ugly beside him, but she did. "I think I need another class," she mumbled. "As far as relaxation went, that one didn't work."

"Is that why you do it, for relaxation?" He couldn't help but notice that many of her classmates, now scattering in various directions, were heavier than she was. Corinne certainly didn't exercise for weight control.

"Yes."

"Okay, then," he said, picking up the pace, "let's walk for a while before we get that coffee."

To her amazement, they did just that. They didn't talk, just walked, briskly, at first, then more leisurely as her tension began to dissipate. Corey seemed attuned to her mood, slowing gradually and comfortably.

By the time they'd reached the coffee shop, Corinne had resolved that, as there was nothing she could do about her appearance, she'd have to live with it. So she straightened her shoulders and tipped up her head and acted as though looking like a slob was *the* way to look.

Corey was smiling as he urged her into a booth, then slid onto the bench opposite her. "Feeling better?"

"Yes," she said, and meant it, if begrudgingly.

"I'm glad." Drawing menus from where they'd been sandwiched between the napkin holder and the sugar, he handed her one, then studied his own. "Any recommendations?"

"The coffee is great here."

"What about something solid?"

"The corn muffins are homemade."

"How about some protein?"

"Are you a health nut?"

"No. Just hungry."

"In that case—" she waved for the waitress, "—I'll order for both of us." And she did. "We'll have two large orange juices with ice, two cheese omelets with sides of bacon, a pair of bagels—is the cream cheese fresh?" At the waitress's nod, she went on. "Then we'll have cream cheese on the bagels and two cups of brewed decaf."

Corey, who was mildly stunned that such a small thing like Corinne planned to match him bite for bite, wasn't to be outdone. "How about those corn muffins?" he asked the waitress.

"Fresh from the oven."

"Add a couple to the order, then." He grinned. "Thank you."

When the waitress had left, Cori stared at him. "You're going to eat all that?"

"What's a little corn muffin on top of everything else you ordered?"

"A little corn muffin here is the equivalent of three elsewhere, and what I ordered is my usual. In the last hour I've burned off at least five hundred calories. What's your excuse?"

"Jogging around the roof track at the hotel?" he asked in a tone of such wishful thinking that the truth was obvious.

"You didn't jog."

"No. But I took a long walk, and just now I walked with you. Anyway, I'm bigger than you are, so I need that many more calories to sustain me."

Only too aware of how much bigger he was, she said nothing. Instead she sat back in the booth and waited patiently. Her lips rested lightly together. Her eyes said, "Okay. You wanted to talk. Go ahead."

"Cute place," he commented, tearing his gaze from hers to scan the surroundings. "Do you come here often?"

"Sometimes, with women from the class. They order the muffin, too." She didn't crack a smile, even when he chuckled.

"I noticed that. I mean, some of them looked a little . . ."

She simply nodded.

"Are you really baby-sitting?"

"Yes."

"Is it a regular job?"

"No, a favor."

"Ah, someone's baby-sitter finked out."

"Actually, it's a favor for me. I like the kids."

He remembered Alan saying that she was good with Scott and Jennifer. "You're sitting for Alan and Julie?"

"I think they're old enough to take care of themselves."

"You know what I mean," he growled.

"No, I'm not sitting for Scott and Jenny. This is another friend. She has three little ones, an absentee husband and not a minute to herself unless she pays for it."

"Tell me you don't charge her."

"I don't charge her."

"Bad business, Cori."

"Good friendship, Corey. And great kids."

"If they're so great, why don't you have some of your own?"

"Because I don't have a husband."

"Why not?"

"I don't want one."

"I see. Your work is your life."

"In part. There are other things I enjoy."

"Like baking?"

Puzzled, she frowned at him.

"Congo bars. They were good."

She arched a brow. "They were for Scott."

"He didn't even know I took the first, and then he offered me a second on his own. I snitched a third after he went to bed."

"That wasn't very nice."

"I was hungry," he said. "Okay. You bake. What else do you enjoy?"

"Friends. Aerobics." She shifted her gaze as the waitress approached. "Cheese omelets."

Corey felt stymied. If he'd hoped that a rumpled and relaxed Corinne was going to soften and open up, he'd been overly optimistic. Her guard was in place—

a wall of composure three feet thick. He wasn't quite sure how to breach it.

As he ate he considered his options in silence. He'd tried charm, but she was impervious to it. The bullying approach had won him an hour of her time, but it hadn't made a crack in that wall. What he needed to do, he realized, was to affect her in such a way that she didn't know she was being affected. For whatever reasons, she'd chosen to think the worst of him. He'd simply have to change that way of thinking before he could begin to make headway with her.

He set down his fork. "That was good." He'd finished the omelet. The juice and bagels were gone. Only the muffin remained. Corinne had been right; it was huge. He cut it and lifted a third, but without taking a bite started to talk. "It's not often that I sit down and have breakfast like this. I'm not usually that great in the morning—always in a rush to get somewhere."

She was eating more leisurely than he had and was still working on her omelet, but he saw that she was listening.

"I live in South Carolina," he went on. "Hilton Head. Have you ever been there?"

She shook her head.

"It's really beautiful. Self-contained and carefully designed. The landscaping on the plantations isn't to be believed. Wild sea oats, palmetto trees, huge live oaks with Spanish moss dangling from their limbs." He warmed easily to the subject. He loved the place and hoped to convey that.

"I have a house on one of the plantations.... Actually, the plantations aren't plantations in the sense of antebellum mansions and cotton gins and landed gentry, but large planned communities that have been built in the past twenty years. My house is in Sea Pines, on the toe of the island, and the road that leads to it is my favorite. What with the lower shrubbery and the oaks and the moss, you feel like you're passing through a tunnel that's lush and alive, a tunnel that changes constantly with the nuances of weather and time of day. Sunset is my favorite time," he said, his eyes distant and a faint smile on his lips. "When the sun gets low enough, it beams right through the tunnel, gilding everything in its path."

"Blinding everything, too," Corinne remarked. "It's tough to drive into the sun."

"But if the sun's at your back, it's like the rays are the energy that propels you forward. You can sit in your car and imagine you're on another planet, far in the future. The sun is driving you, the trees are guiding you, and there's nothing but heaven on the horizon."

The picture he painted was so real she could almost see it. "It must be a letdown when you emerge from the tunnel."

"Mmm." He took a healthy bite of the muffin, then had to wait until he'd swallowed to speak again. "But my house is some consolation. It's peaceful. It's cool and shaded. It's at the end of a private way, so I don't see other cars or people. If I go out on the deck, close my eyes and listen to the rustle of the leaves, I can almost pretend I really am in paradise."

"Are you dissatisfied with the world we have?" she asked a little tartly. It wasn't that she wanted to know his feelings, she told herself, simply that she was defensive of her own time and place.

"Not dissatisfied. I like this world. I really do. But it's fun to imagine other worlds." He gave a soft snort. "Maybe I read too much science fiction."

Corinne had never read science fiction. Nonfiction was more her style. History fascinated her, as did the fact of history repeating itself. It always amazed her that civilizations could make the same mistakes over and over again. She was determined not to do that in her own tiny breath of life.

"Anyway," Corey was saying with a sigh, "my own world is pretty hectic, which is why stolen hours like this are a treat."

"If you're an executive who leaves most of the work to his managers, why are things so hectic?"

"I leave most of the *managing* to managers. There are still dozens of decisions to be made in the course of a day."

"Once you buy a hotel and get it running, what's to be done?" she asked in a way that could have made the question rhetorical. She didn't want Corey to think she was interested, yet she was pleased when he answered.

"There are policies to be set and then altered when something becomes an issue—like security or convention policy or complimentary services. There are decisions to be made on renovation and expansion, and there's a tone to be set. The maids take cues from their supervisors, the supervisors from the management and the management from me. I'm the one who decides that every visitor is to be treated with respect, or it doesn't happen."

"Is that what you demand at your hotels?"

"Yes. If people pay good money, they deserve good service."

"Or they won't come back, so it's a wise business move." She didn't want to think that the standards he set were out of the goodness of his heart. She didn't want to think there was any goodness in his heart.

Corey gestured to the waitress and pointed to his drained coffee cup. "How about you, Cori? A refill?"

She glanced at her watch. She had another fifteen minutes. "Why not," she said with a light shrug.

"Don't worry," he chided, but with a half smile that slashed a roguish crease in his cheek, "you'll be out of here in time. I may not be great about punctuality when it's just me, but where others are concerned, I'm pretty good. Then again—" his brow creased, as though he were trying to figure it out "—maybe it's *because* of others that I'm often late. I like being with people. I forget the time."

"You must be with people more often than not."

"I am. That's what's so great about my job. I don't think I could bear being a computer programmer or an artist or a writer. Having myself for company twenty-four hours a day would be trying."

"I can believe that."

He scowled. "You twist my words. Do you know that?"

"There wasn't any twisting involved. I simply responded to what you said."

"But you take everything so literally. What I meant was that I'd be bored if I didn't have outside stimulation. Human stimulation."

"A psychiatrist would say that you're not comfortable with yourself."

Arms resting casually on the table, he sat back. "Do I look like I'm not?"

She thought he looked positively smug and incredibly arrogant. "I'm not a psychiatrist."

"In your lay opinion, what do you think?"

"I think that you've convinced yourself you are. I think that a hefty ego covers a multitude of sins."

"I don't have a hefty ego—okay, don't look at me that way—maybe I do have an ego, but it's not hefty and what there is of it I've earned. I've done a lot with my life and I'm proud of it. I wasn't born with a silver spoon in my mouth, but my kids will be."

"You plan on having kids?"

"Shouldn't I?"

She moved her head in a dismissive gesture. "You've had plenty of time, but it hasn't happened yet."

"I'm careful. I protect my women." It was the wrong thing to say. He knew it the minute the words left his mouth. To recoup...to recoup...somehow the truth seemed the wisest course, so that was what he offered, with no trace of a smile. "For the past fourteen years I've worked hard at being successful. And just as I've worked hard, I've played hard. There have been women in my life, Corinne. Lots of them. But it would have been just as wrong to subject any one of them to the running around I do for work, as it would have been to pretend I was in love. I've never said those words to a woman. For whatever other faults I have, I've been scrupulously honest in relationships. I've never promised a thing that I haven't delivered. Someday—" he paused, frowning for an instant "—someday the right woman will come along. *Then* I'll think of having kids."

Corinne didn't want to hear him. Not only that, but she didn't want to hear him speak with such intensity, such . . . sincerity.

"That's a very noble attitude," she answered flippantly. "I'm sure the right woman will be thrilled."

Corey pressed the creases on his brow, then wearily drew his hand down his face. His gaze met hers, demanding attention. "What is it about me that rubs you the wrong way? Can't you give me credit for anything? I've been hoping to show you that I'm not the ogre you think I am, but nothing I do or say makes any difference. What *is* it about me that bugs you so?"

"Nothing," she lied. "You're fine."

He bowed his head and shook it. " 'Fine.' That's great, just great." His eyes rose to pin hers. "Okay, if I'm fine, how about going out with me tonight?"

"I can't."

"You have plans. Why didn't I think of that first?" He made no effort to hide his sarcasm. He was frustrated enough to forget about the white gloves he was supposed to be wearing.

Corinne remained entirely composed—which annoyed him all the more—but that didn't prevent her, white gloves and all, from voicing her opinion. "You think what you want and act on what you think. You don't stop to consider that I may want to think and act differently. You won't take no for an answer."

" 'No,' as in you don't want to go out with me?"

"That's right."

"Ever?"

"Ever."

"A psychiatrist would have something to say about that," he mocked.

"I already know what a psychiatrist would say and frankly I don't care. Maybe we do have one similarity, you and I. I, too, think what I want and act on what I think. Unfortunately, what *I* think is very different from what *you* think."

"So we're stalemated."

"Looks that way."

Corey eyed the rest of his muffin with distaste. He stretched sideways to dig into a pocket for his wallet. "Have you had enough?"

"Yes."

"Come on." He tossed his head toward the door as he slid from the booth. "Let's get out of here." Dropping a more than adequate number of bills on the table, he waited for Corinne to stand, then followed her out to the street. "Where's your car?"

She'd no sooner pointed when he took her elbow and started in that direction. He dropped his hand seconds later, though, and they walked in silence. She gnawed on the inside of her mouth and cast intermittent glances his way, but his head was down, eyes on the sidewalk ahead of him.

When they'd reached her car she opened the door, then turned. "I'm sorry, Corey," she said softly. "It's not you. It's me. I've built the kind of life I have because it's what I need. I need to be structured and organized. I need to have my feet on firm ground. I need to be in control. There are some things I can't handle, so I avoid them at all costs. You," she said, sighing, "I can't handle."

Her tone was so gentle that he wanted to scream. Instead he spoke carefully, leashing his frustration. "How can you know if you don't try me?"

"I know. I know myself."

"I'm not a menace," he ventured defensively. "It's not like I'd tear you apart limb by limb."

"I know that."

"Then what is it? Why won't you give me a chance?"

"Why would you *want* a chance?" she cried, as frustrated now as he. "What are you wasting your time on me for? I'm not dynamic. I'm not colorful or flamboyant or captivating. Why are you *toying* with me?"

"I'm not toying with you," he said very quietly.

"What would you call it?"

"I'd call it...ah, hell, it doesn't matter what I'd call it." If she wouldn't see him, she wouldn't see him. Defeat wasn't something he accepted graciously. Gesturing toward the driver's seat, he waited for her to slide in, then closed the door.

To his surprise, she rolled down the window. "Thanks for the breakfast."

"Anytime. Take care."

She hesitated, her gaze steady on him. "Do you need a lift somewhere?"

"I have a rental car."

Still she hesitated, but only for a moment longer. Then, with a single nod, she started the car and drove off.

Once Corey's frustration eased, he realized that he hadn't been as unsuccessful as he'd thought. He'd wanted to talk with Cori, to get to know her, and in some ways he had. The details of her life remained a mystery, as did the underlying force that made her the way she was. One thing he'd learned, though, was that she wasn't as indifferent to him as she wanted to believe. *Why are you toying with me?* she'd asked, implying that she felt he was tempting her with something she couldn't have. To be tempted, one had to want. The question was why she felt she couldn't have what she wanted.

Then again, the question was why Corey wanted *her*. He knew now that he did. Something in the pit of his stomach stirred when he thought of her, and it wasn't indigestion.

She'd looked adorable just now, trying to appear dignified in her sweats. The color had remained in her cheeks throughout breakfast—pale pink patches that were delightful. Her hair had dried, and if, as he guessed, she'd have liked to run off and comb it, she'd resisted the urge. Without earrings the delicacy of her lobes was exposed. And he'd noticed that she had a small bump on the bridge of her nose; it probably drove her crazy, but he thought it added character. Hidden character. Just as, he suspected, those brown eyes could express many different emotions if she allowed them to.

Then, too, he remembered the moments they'd spent in the corridor of her office. When he'd leaned close he'd felt the softness of her cheek and the gentle brush of her hair. He'd smelled something light, lemony but sweet—not perfume, she wasn't the type, but perhaps soap or shampoo—and it had tantalized him with the same understated quality that characterized the woman herself.

His fingers had curled around arms that were slender but solid. His chest had brushed against breasts that were small but firm. He'd pressed himself—for a fleeting moment, yet that had been enough—against hips that were slim but promising.

Slender . . . firm . . . promising. Yes, he wanted her. But there was something else, something in her character that fascinated him. He'd had his first glimpse of it during those brief moments at the car, when she hadn't quite wanted to send him away without explaining herself. There was a sensitive side to her, a side that had felt badly because she'd hurt him. That encouraged him.

And there was a vulnerability about her verging on fragility. That appealed to him tremendously, partly because he'd never met a woman with that quality, partly because it brought out a protectiveness in him that he'd never felt before.

He'd known all along that Corinne was different. He'd known that she'd command a different approach. Now, as he began to understand the ways in which she was different, he could better comprehend the type of approach he'd need to take.

Many questions remained, their answers as elusive as ever. But of one thing he was sure. Regardless of what Corinne Fremont chose to believe, he certainly wasn't done with her.

# 3

A week later, when Corey returned to Baltimore, he went directly to Alan's office. He'd even had his secretary call ahead for an appointment. After all, this was business.

"Business?" Alan asked.

"Business," Corey answered. "I want your firm to do a survey for me. Actually, not for me alone. For a group of developers on Hilton Head." It had all been so easy. He'd been prepared to twist a few arms or, if necessary, finance the survey on his own. The expenditure wouldn't have bothered him in the least, though he knew there would be more legitimacy to the contract if he was but one of several signers. As it happened, he hadn't had to twist a single arm. The people he'd approached had been totally amenable to the project.

"I have one hotel on the island," he went on, "plus several condominium complexes in the works. Other hotel owners are in similar situations. We feel that it would be beneficial, before we commit ourselves even further, to survey visitors to the island and find out what they want, what they don't want, why they've come, whether they'd return and so on."

Alan pursed his lips. "Why now, all of a sudden?"

"Now, because the summer season's approaching and the number of potential respondents will be the greatest. Fear of terrorism is keeping many people away from Europe, which means they'll be looking for vacation alternatives. That business could be lucrative. We have a lot to gain if we can offer what travelers want."

"All of a sudden?" Alan prodded, buying Corey's explanation only up to a point.

"All of a sudden—" Corey shrugged. "Because I didn't think of it before."

"What made you think of it now?"

The speculative look in Alan's eye held its share of suspicion. Corey knew his friend was sharp, but Corey was no slouch, himself. He'd thought everything out, from demands to explanations, and particularly given the support of others on Hilton Head, he wasn't about to back down.

"I thought of it now because of Corinne," he said. His gaze was direct and without remorse. "I want her to run the survey."

Alan closed his eyes, lowered his head and shook it. "Corey, Corey, Corey. You don't give up, do you?"

"No."

Raising his head, Alan returned every bit as direct a look as Corey had given him moments before. "I'll do your survey myself. I'm still an active analyst."

"No offense, but I want Corinne."

"Why?"

"Because she's good."

"So am I."

"You're not Corinne."

"And she's the reason you've thought up this scheme."

"Only in part. The other part tells me that the survey would be worthwhile."

"That part I already know. If it hadn't been like taking money from my brother, I'd have suggested it before, myself."

"Money's not the issue, but there is something to be said for the fact that you and I are too close to work together." Alan's skeptical stare goaded him on. "I'm not too close to Corinne."

"Exactly how close are you? You saw her for a few seconds at the house that time, and I got word that you saw her here last week." His voice lowered, accusatory in a teasing way. "You didn't tell me you were in, Corey."

Corey waved a hand. "I was in and out. Just wanted to say hello."

"Not to me."

"You were busy. I didn't want to disturb you."

"And Corinne wasn't busy?" he asked rhetorically, then leaned back in his chair and linked his fingers over his middle. "Go on. I'd like to hear what happened."

"Nothing happened."

"That I can believe. You won't get anywhere with Corinne."

Corey wasn't about to tell Alan about the time he'd spent with her on Saturday morning. Apparently Alan didn't know, which meant that Corinne hadn't told him, which meant that she hadn't run to him for rescue. But then, Corey had suspected all along that she could take care of herself.

"Corinne," Corey stated, "is a businesswoman through and through. That's one of the reasons I'd like her to do the survey."

"And the other reasons?"

"She'd impress everyone at Hilton Head. She'd fit in more easily among the guests than you would. She'd be able to spend the time there that she needs, whereas you have other commitments here."

"You're right about that," Alan admitted. "I don't do location assignments myself unless I have to. As it is, I travel too much for Julie's peace of mind. And mine. I admit it. I like being with Julie and the kids."

"And I admire you for it, Alan. There's no need to get defensive. But Corinne doesn't have a husband and kids. Other than her grandmother, there's no one to keep her here."

"I need her here. She's a critical cog in the wheel of this organization. If you think I can let her go running off for the summer..."

It was Corey's turn to chide. "Is Corinne the type to go running off for the summer?" he asked, then went on without waiting for an answer. "She's not, and I wouldn't ask it of her. I'm talking two weeks here, two weeks there. Isn't that how your analysts work? They can't do it all from the office."

"No, but..." His voice trailed off and his eyes narrowed. "There's something you're not saying, something personal that's behind all this."

"What could be personal?"

"Asked a little too innocently."

"But I'm serious. You've said it yourself—Corinne isn't my kind of girl."

"That didn't seem to faze you when we talked last. You wanted to get to know her, you said, and you left the outcome open-ended."

"Look," Corey drawled, "I can't promise the woman won't fall in love with me."

Alan's laugh was a full-throated one. "Corinne? That'll be the day."

"If you're so sure of it," Corey replied, vaguely bothered, "what's the problem? I want her to do my survey because she's good and she's available."

"Who said anything about being available? She's working on half a dozen other projects right now. I told you. I need her here."

"Maybe available is the wrong word. She isn't tied down to a family. Is that better? Better still, look at it this way. If I were a guy coming in off the street wanting to hire your firm to do a study, you'd consider Corinne for the assignment, wouldn't you?"

"I'd have to check out my analysts' schedules."

"Come on, Alan. You only have three, besides yourself, and if Cori is so valuable to you, it's because she's better than the others, and I want the best, so why not Cori?"

"I do not trust you."

"What's not to *trust*?"

Alan sent a helpless glance skyward, then dropped it to the framed picture of Julie and the children that sat on the corner of his desk. "We've been there together, Corey. We've competed for women, even shared them on occasion. We may have gone our separate ways after college, but we kept in touch enough to know that we still shared a certain wildness. It was that way with me right up to the day seven years ago when I met Julie." He shrugged. "Maybe I was sowing my wild oats knowing that once she came along things would be different. Maybe I was simply floundering. But whatever the cause, I know how I was, and I wouldn't wish that on Corinne for all the tea in China."

"You're trying to protect her. I hear you, Alan, and I respect what you're saying. What *I'm* saying is that I've grown up, too. I may not have married like you did, but neither am I the way we both were seven years ago, and even if I were, I'd have to be deaf, dumb and blind not to realize that Corinne isn't a woman to fool with. I've already told you I won't hurt her. What more can I do to convince you?"

"Turn around and take your business elsewhere?" Alan offered, tongue-in-cheek.

"I can't do that."

Somehow Alan had known he'd say that. Somehow, perhaps because the two men had shared so much and were so alike, he did believe that Corey wouldn't knowingly hurt Corinne. Moreover, something had crept into Corey's expression that was serious and intense, even vulnerable. That look reminded Alan of the very things he'd felt when he'd first set eyes on Julie. For the first time it occurred to him that Corinne might prove to be exactly what Corey Haraden needed.

The thought brought a smile to his face. He liked the idea of his best friend getting together with a woman he cherished like a sister. And if it didn't work out, he mused with growing enthusiasm for the possibilities, one thing was for sure—Corey would be given a run for his money.

"Okay," he said smugly. "You're on."

"I am?" Corey asked.

"Yup."

"And Corinne can do the survey?"

"I'll have to check it out with her first. If she can spare the time, she's yours."

While not one to look a gift horse in the mouth, Corey couldn't help but be suspicious. "Why the turnabout?"

Alan grinned. "It's suddenly occurred to me that Corinne may not be the one in danger here."

"Meaning what?"

"Meaning that she'll be a tough nut to crack—mind you, a lovable one, but tough. It could be that you'll be the one to end up a little bruised."

"Hell, I only want her to work for me."

"Right. So, why don't we put it to her now. I'm pretty sure she's in." He reached for the phone, but Corey stopped him.

"Wait. Maybe you ought to talk with her alone."

Alan was amused by what sounded suspiciously like nervousness. "Why? If you two are going to be working together . . ."

"She . . . may want to discuss it with you or think about it. She knows we're friends, you and I. I wouldn't want to put her on the spot."

"You think she'll refuse?"

"To work with me?" He didn't only think it; he feared it. "Of course not. But if she does have certain . . . reservations, you can set her straight."

"It's not every woman who gets a chance to work with the Cardinal, eh?"

"Something like that," Corey said, craning his neck against a tie that suddenly seemed too tight.

"Tell me one last thing," Alan asked. "If I'd outright turned you down, would you have gone to another firm?"

Corey thought about that for a minute, but just then he was feeling defensive enough to be brash. "Not on your life. It's Corinne or nothing."

* * *

Corinne was more than ready to vote for the "nothing" when Alan broached the idea of the project to her that afternoon. Nevertheless, she kept her personal feelings in check and chose her words with care.

"The idea of a survey is good," she admitted. "We both know it could provide useful information. Has anything like it been done before on Hilton Head?"

"Not to my knowledge."

"Who else is involved, besides your friend?" She was pleased with the nonpersonal way she'd phrased the question. She wasn't sure if Alan knew of the times she'd seen Corey, but even if he did, she didn't want him to think there was anything going on.

"I don't have the other names," Alan answered. "Corey referred to developers with interests similar to his—hotels, condominiums, that kind of thing. I know that there are a slew of stores and restaurants down there. I'm sure those owners would stand to benefit from increased tourism, but I doubt they're big enough to contribute to the kitty."

Corinne nodded. She smoothed the pad of her thumb over the gently rounded nail of her forefinger. "You could handle this one yourself, Alan."

Alan shook his head. "He wants you."

What else is new? "Did he say why?"

"He said that he and I are too close, and that I have too many other commitments, and I suppose he's right. He also said that he thinks you're the best, and I know he's right there."

Though her expression didn't betray a thing, Corinne marveled at Corey Haraden's gall. She'd actually felt sorry for him on Saturday morning. She'd actually felt guilty for having rebuffed him. She'd tried to explain herself to him and had hoped he'd accept it. Obviously he hadn't. *He thinks you're the best.*

"Flattery will get him nowhere," she mumbled, then realizing what she'd done, she shifted uncomfortably in her seat. "Uh, Alan, I don't think I really want to work for him. I know he's a good friend of yours, but couldn't one of the others do the survey?"

"He asked for you."

"I know, but that doesn't mean he has to get me. I have so much other work to do. . . ."

"Most of which should be cleared up in the next few weeks."

"But just last week two new projects came in."

"And you'll be able to work them in around this one."

"But this one will be time-consuming. We're not talking day trips here; Hilton Head isn't the easiest of commutes. If the project's to be done right, I'd have to be there for days at a time."

Alan had to keep from smiling as he watched her grope for excuses. She was so poised and prim, with only her eyes revealing an inner qualm; she made an adorable picture. He guessed that Corey had made as much of an impression on Corinne as she'd made on him, which reinforced Alan's decision to let them have a go at each other. Granted, Corinne didn't want that, but he had faith in her.

He'd seen something in Corey's eyes when they'd been talking earlier, something raw and helpless. The Cardinal had been a freewheeler for a long time, perhaps too long. It could just be that he was looking for a place to light.

Corinne was strong. Vulnerable, in some ways, but strong. The more Alan thought about it, the more he knew that if anyone could handle Corey it was her.

"It wouldn't be that bad," he said with a negligent wave of his hand. "Actually, I envy you. It'll be gorgeous down there in the summer."

"It's gorgeous up here. And if we're talking vacations, I already have mine planned." Two weeks at a small Vermont inn in August. She'd made reservations three months before.

"We're talking work, Cori."

"Yes."

"Does he make you nervous?"

"Nervous?" Her voice wavered. With a determined effort she steadied it. "Why would he make me nervous?"

Alan rubbed a finger along his jaw as he considered the question. "I can think of several reasons."

"Like his looks? Or his style? Or the fact that he's aggressive, persistent, arrogant and annoying?"

"How did you know all that?"

"I . . . intuition," she said quickly. She had the distinct feeling that Alan was amused, and while she saw nothing amusing in the prospect of entering into a close working relationship with Corey Haraden, she was still a professional. It was as such that she offered a very professional opinion. "I think we'd have trouble working together."

"Oh?"

"We're both opinionated. I'm afraid we'd lock horns."

"This is *work*, Cori. We've had tough clients and you've never been fazed. Corey won't be a problem." In the matter of work, at least, he added silently.

But those very same silent words were screaming through Corinne's mind. Slowly she shook her head. "I don't think it's such a good idea."

"How about you look at it as a direct assignment from me."

"I've talked my way out of direct assignments before." Indeed, she had, but rarely and only in the extreme case where the nature of the project had gone against her principles. Unfortunately, there was nothing about Corey Haraden's proposal, per se, that went against her principles. The look in Alan's eye told her that he knew it, too.

"How about you consider it a favor for me," he coaxed.

"Because Corey's a friend?"

"Yes. His money's as green as anyone else's, and you can be sure that he'll pay, but there's a matter of my pride involved. I'd like to give him the best we've got."

"Flattery won't get *you* anywhere, either," she pointed out dryly.

"Then how about this. How about you look on the job as a challenge. Do you think you can handle it? Do you think you can handle as aggressive, persistent, arrogant and annoying a client as Corey Haraden and do the kind of job I've come to expect of you?"

Deliberately and without remorse, Alan had presented the one argument he knew stood a chance. Yes, there was a half smile on his face, but there was a definite dare in his eyes that went a step beyond humor. While Corinne hadn't been moved to cater to his pride, her own pride was another matter. In the five years she'd been with him, it had been one of her greatest sources of strength. She prided herself on tackling the trickiest of cases and dealing with the most persnickety of clients, and even more, she prided herself on doing her job well.

"Dirty pool," she muttered with an uncharacteristic twist of her lips.

"Is that a yes?"

"Yes, it's a yes." She took a deep breath and let it linger in her lungs long enough to make her a little light-headed. "I've handled aggressive clients before."

"They're not Corey," he taunted in a singsong tone.

"I've handled persistent and arrogant and annoying clients, too."

He repeated the refrain. "They're not Corey."

"I can *handle* Corey. Okay?"

Alan knew that he'd backhandedly forced her into it. He knew that if he suddenly changed his mind and withdrew the offer, she'd argue. Pride was a marvelous thing, he mused, and sat back with a smug smile. "Are you sure?"

She didn't bother to answer. She didn't even want to think of the question. She'd been railroaded, and she knew it. She also knew that one part of her wasn't totally upset with the outcome, though she didn't want to think deeply on that, either. "What's the schedule?" she asked, moving ahead before she could shy back.

Alan was all for moving ahead, too. "Corey will be here in the morning. You can sit down with him then and discuss the details of the project. My guess is that he'll want you to check out the setup on Hilton Head, maybe meet the other people in his group before you work anything up. Take a look at your schedule and see when you can go. Also, you may want to take a look at the Marriott project we did several years back. We ran into a couple of snafus with our sample. I think you can improve on it this time around.''

Corinne was making mental notes, adding several others to what Alan had said. She would be fine, she realized, as long as her mind was on work. The project appealed to her. The location appealed to her. The fact that the principal client could prove to be a thorn in her side was secondary to the task at hand. She'd handled thorns before, and she'd handle this one. Corey Haraden was a challenge that she would meet head-on and conquer. As long as she stood firm in her convictions, she was unprickable.

By the time the receptionist announced Corey's arrival the next morning, Corinne was prepared for battle. For armor, she wore a gray business suit replete with stiff collar and necktie. For war paint, she'd applied dark eye shadow and mascara, a spot of blusher and a rim of lip gloss. And as for state of mind, she'd spent half the night gearing herself up for the nastiest of confrontations.

Unfortunately, Corey didn't look terribly fierce when he strolled into her office. He was wearing a pair of light gray slacks, a tweed blazer and loafers. His tie was endearingly crooked.

Nor did he look smug, and as that was one of the things she'd been prepared to fight, some of the wind left her sails then and there. The smile on his face was friendly, infectious. It was all she could do not to return it.

''Alan tells me you've accepted the job,'' he announced buoyantly. ''I'm really glad.''

She cleared her throat. ''He was very persuasive. A little biased, perhaps, but persuasive.'' She was sitting behind her desk, having doubted the wisdom of jumping up to shake his hand. Suddenly she wondered if she was being impolite. War was one thing; social laxity another. She had no intention of being faulted on either. "Please, have a seat."

With a minimum of movement he settled into the chair facing her. He put his elbows on the arms and linked his fingers. "So," he said quietly, "where do we begin?"

*You had no right doing this to me! You knew I didn't want to work with you, mix with you, have anything to do with you! You're an arrogant cad, do you know that?* "You could start by telling me what you had in mind. I know what you told Alan, but it would help if I heard it from the horse's mouth."

"Do I really remind you of a horse?"

Oh, yes. A magnificent stallion. "That was a figure of speech. I'm sorry."

Corey let it go at that. He could see that she was itching for a fight—something about the way her small chin was set—and he was determined not to goad her. He wanted them to get off on the right foot this time around. He was sure they could walk in step with each other. He was *sure* of it. He, for one, was more than willing to slow his pace to match hers.

So he repeated what he'd told Alan about the survey he wanted done and why, leaving out, of course, the part about her involvement being an absolute prerequisite. "We need information for future planning," he concluded. "Think you can get us some?"

"I know I can. It's my job," she said, then went on to paraphrase the credo he'd offered the Saturday before. "If you pay good money, you get good service. I assume you've already worked out a fee with Alan."

"Actually, no. I'll pay what it costs. I want the job done well, which is why I came here."

"Oh?"

"Yes, oh. Now, about that information..."

Corinne was feeling waspish, and ashamed of herself for it. Corey was behaving in a pleasant enough manner, carrying on as though there had never been a dissonant chord between them. Taking a breath, she followed his example. "I'll need to know as much as I can about Hilton Head. I've already done some reading—"

"When did you do that?"

"Last night."

He dipped his head in admiration. "Not bad, Cori."

"Not good, Corey. The library didn't have much, I'm afraid—a paragraph or two in a travel guide, an article or two in a magazine."

"No sweat. I can send you a bunch of stuff. Better still, you can come down and take the Cook's tour yourself."

She knew he was testing her. It wasn't in his eyes, or his voice; he seemed totally relaxed and sincere. But she *knew* he was testing her. He wanted to see whether she'd chicken out of making a trip for the sake of research alone. "A visit would be ideal," she said smoothly. "That way I can see what the island has to offer firsthand. I'd also like to talk with the others in the group backing this project. I'll be forming ideas of my own as we go along, but I'll need to know exactly what you all want to learn from the survey."

He nodded. "I'll arrange it. Give me a date—we can do it in a day, though two or three would be better— and I'll set it all up."

*He thinks I'll take the coward's way out and pick a single day a month from now*, she mused, as she took her calendar from the top right desk drawer. "How about next Wednesday?" That was only five days off. *Are you mad, Corinne? There's no way you can clear things up by then, not to mention preparing yourself mentally.* "I could fly down early in the day, which would give us the rest of Wednesday, plus Thursday, Friday and Saturday." *You are mad!* She looked up innocently. "If you're free, of course."

Corey was ecstatic, but he spoke in an evenly modulated voice. "I'll be free. I'll phone my secretary later and have her air express a packet of information to you, so you'll have a chance to thumb through it, if not before, then on the plane ride down. Shall I have her make the flight arrangements?"

"No need. I can do it from this end."

Drawing a card from the inside pocket of his blazer, he leaned forward to set it on the desk. "Give us a call when your plans are firm. We'll have a car waiting to pick you up in Savannah. It's an easy forty-five-minute drive from there."

She left the card where it lay, but reached for a pencil. "That sounds fine."

"Well, then." He smiled gently and stood. "I guess we're all set for now."

She was making notations on her calendar. "I think so. If I have any questions between now and then, I'll call. Otherwise, I'll see you next Wednesday." *Mad! Utterly mad!*

Corey thought of politely extending his hand, then thought again. Yes, he wanted to feel the slenderness of her fingers, the smoothness of her skin. Yes, he wanted that small physical contact. But he'd deliberately worked to make this meeting short, swift and innocent, and he wasn't at all sure he could hold her hand in any manner that would be short, swift or innocent. Not after sitting before her, listening to the mellowness of her voice, absorbing the brown depth of her gaze, being aware—if only peripherally, as he hadn't dared look directly—of the gentle rise and fall of her breasts beneath her layers of clothing. He was hot looking at her, but she was as cool and composed as ever. He wanted her hot, too, but not now, not now. Soon enough, when she was on his turf.

Burying his hands in his pockets for safekeeping, he simply smiled again. "I'll see you then," he said quietly, and turned and left.

Corinne stared at the empty doorway long after he'd gone. Tremors rippled through her stomach, but she quelled them in a surge of anger.

He was too nice.

*He was trying to be polite.*

He was trying to trick me. It's a trap. I know it is.

*You're too suspicious.*

Suspicion is a strength. I have to be on my guard.

*But didn't he look good? Admit it. He's gorgeous.*

He's dangerous.

*When he reached out to set down his card, did you get a look at the little bits of soft brown hair just above his wrist?*

No, I did not. And they were auburn, not brown.

*How about that smile? Gentle and friendly. And the dimples it put on his cheeks? I'll bet he shaves twice a day.*

You'll never know. You won't get close enough. This is a test. That's all it is.

*Mmm. And an enticing one at that.*

It's a test of my strength. I'll prove to myself, and to him, that I can keep him at arm's length.

*Is that where you intend to keep him? Bo-ring.*

Pru-dent. He's a menace.

*But a tempting one, don't you think?*

I am not tempted. You'll see.

And with that she upended her pencil and diligently erased the nonsensical scratchings she'd made on her calendar.

The car waiting to meet Corinne in Savannah was low-slung, black and Corey's. She'd half suspected it would be, but that didn't keep her from having to deal with annoyance, as well as a rush of heat. Late May in Baltimore was warm enough. Georgia was worse. She wondered what it would be like in the lowlands of South Carolina, then wondered if she'd melt when Corey straightened from where he'd been leaning against the car and came toward her.

He was wearing casual pants, lightly pleated at the waist, and a stylishly oversize short-sleeved pullover. Auburn-haired, green-eyed and smiling, he quickly reached for her bag and slung it over his shoulder to walk her the rest of the way to the car.

"How was the flight?"

"Fine. Very smooth, actually."

"You're right on time. There mustn't have been any delay in Atlanta."

"No."

"You lucked out. Did they feed you?"

"Breakfast." Not that she'd eaten much. She wondered if she was coming down with something. Her stomach was jumpy.

"We'll grab some lunch when we get to the island." Opening the passenger's door, he stowed her bag in the small space behind the seats, then stood aside while she slid in as gracefully as possible, which was no mean feat given the lowness of the car.

Tucking her pocketbook neatly by her feet, she crossed her legs, then smoothed the cotton duck of her pants. They were white. She made a quick inspection for dirt, found one smudge of dust and brushed it off. She barely had time to straighten her blouse—slate blue and nowhere near as cool as she'd have liked— before Corey was folding himself behind the wheel. Without pause, he turned on the engine and adjusted the air-conditioning, sending a stream of cool air through the car.

"That feels good," she breathed, reaching for the seat belt. "I wasn't prepared for the heat." Lord only knew she'd had enough else on her mind preparing herself for this trip.

"Not to worry. Everything's air-conditioned except the beach, and the water's always refreshing." He watched for a minute while she adjusted the seat belt so that it lay in a neat diagonal between her breasts. She couldn't possibly know how the strap molded her shape, making her breasts look fuller, hinting at a covering of lace. If she did, he mused, he doubted she'd be sitting in such a self-possessed way.

Swallowing a sigh, he glanced in his rearview mirror, backed the car around and headed from the terminal. "Did you get the things I sent?"

"Yes. Thank you. They were informative."

So formal, he mused. He was going to have to work on that, gently. "I've set up meetings with several of the other hotel owners and a few shopkeepers. They can give you ideas about things they'd like to know, but my guess is that you'll get inspiration just listening to them discuss their experiences here. You'll be able to dream up angles we haven't thought of."

She nodded. He was being considerate and insightful, the ideal client. Too considerate. What did he have up his sleeve? Too insightful. Could he tell that she hadn't slept well for the past five nights, and that she was as annoyed about that as she was about the way his lean fingers curved so gracefully around the steering wheel?

Focusing on the view beyond the windshield, she asked, "This is Savannah? It's more...modest than I'd imagined."

"Diplomatically put. I'd have called it run-down, but this is the city's fringe. Downtown Savannah is modest, but it has charm. There's a large historical area to drive through, and the waterfront has been restored. If you'd like, we could come in for an afternoon and explore."

"That would be nice, if we have time," she said quietly, "but I'd like to make as much headway on the project as possible."

"Do you have a long-range timetable in mind?"

"Do you?"

"I want the information yesterday," he said, and tossed her a teasing grin.

Corinne could do without his teasing, not to mention his grins. They weakened her and she didn't want to be weakened, so she concentrated on work. "If all goes well, I could have the preliminary plans for the survey completed in a week after I return to Baltimore."

"Preliminary plans. You mean the questionnaire itself?"

"Possibly, but there are other decisions to be made first."

"Such as?"

"What form the survey will take."

"What's our choice?"

"In general? There are three options in market research. The first is a telephone survey. We could cull a cold sample from the phone book or a slightly warmer one from the client lists of travel agents, but I don't think either would be optimal here. The second option is a mail-out. Actually, a version of that would probably be our best bet."

"Go on."

"I was thinking of putting printed questionnaires in the rooms of every guest over a specified period of time, say a month. Response would be voluntary. In the past we've used incentives, such as a free drink at the bar in exchange for a completed questionnaire, but something as limited as that appeals mainly to drinkers."

"Don't knock 'em. The bar makes money."

"True, but if we want the broadest sample possible, we'll have to broaden the choice of rewards. Don't ask me the specifics. They'll depend partly on what you're willing to offer—the cost of incentives can add up—and partly on what strikes me once I've seen the hotels."

"What about guests in condominiums?"

"They can be given questionnaires when they check in, perhaps get a small rebate for a completed questionnaire when they check out."

"Not bad."

"Then there's the third option," she went on, her enthusiasm growing with his positive response, and it had been positive. Understated, but positive. "In-person interviews. That's where we get real depth."

"You mean, something beyond yes and no?"

"Uh-huh. Actually, we can go beyond that in a questionnaire, but only to an extent."

"Until the respondent gets writer's cramp," he drawled in such a way that she had to keep her lips from twitching.

"Not exactly what I was thinking, but the effect's the same. There are two types of questions on a printed form. Closed-ended is where the respondent circles a figure pertaining to age group, marital status, number of children, income level. Open-ended is where he—or she—would jot down a note about what he liked best about his stay or what would bring him back again. People will only write so much. If we can follow the questionnaire up with a personal interview, we'll be able to probe further."

Corey was thoroughly enjoying listening to her speak. Not only did she sound competent and confident, but her voice flowed gently. He wondered if she was aware of it, then decided that she wasn't. She was too wrapped up in the telling, which perhaps explained why her tone lacked the edge it had at times. He wasn't about to distract her. "How do you go about arranging for personal interviews?"

"We put a question to that effect on the question-naire."

"Do you set up a meeting right at the hotel?"

"Possibly, but I think I'd rather ask if we could contact the respondent later. It's enough to have him fill out the questionnaire without asking for another little chunk of his vacation time, in addition to which his thoughts will have jelled more once he's back home. We can use the phone for that phase of the study. Needless to say, it'll be a much smaller group than the overall sample, but the responses could be enlightening.''

"Not bad," Corey repeated, this time with a definite lilt. "You've really thought this out, haven't you."

"It's my job."

"Will your job permit you to relax a little while you're down here?"

Here it comes. "Only when I'm *off* the job, which means at night when I'm alone in my room."

"Is that what Alan decrees?"

"It's what I decree," she said, staring straight ahead.

"What about me? Don't I get to decree something? After all, I'm the boss."

She gave a single exaggerated nod, aware that it might be nice to know exactly what she was up against. "Okay. What would you decree?"

He shrugged. "Three meals a day, plus coffee breaks? Maybe a look at the nightlife around. Actually, that'd come under the category of work."

"Oh?"

"Sure. You have to see for yourself what the island has to offer, don't you?"

"Not in the extreme."

"You'd call a band concert or a little dancing or a moonlight walk on the beach the extreme?"

Very, she thought. Oh, the first was innocent enough, but the second and third ... *Trouble, Corinne. Not your style, at least, not with this particular man. He'd be the smoothest of dancers, and he'd hold*

*you seductively close. And on the beach by moon-
light, he'd kick off his shoes, roll up his pants, throw
his arm around your shoulder and whisper sweet
nothings in your ear. Then again, maybe the ocean
would do that, or a midnight breeze, but the outcome
would be the same. You'd freeze up. You'd remember
all the years you'd been alone when the only thing
you'd wanted was your parents, but they hadn't been
there because they'd been off running around, having
the time of their lives with ever-changing partners,
breezing through life without a care in the world.
You'd remember the vow you made one night when
you were twelve, when you had your hands filled with
Roxanne and Gram's demands had been unending and
you'd wanted that awful responsibility taken from
your shoulders, when you decided that you'd never,
never do what your parents had done. You'd remember Tom O'Neill and Richard Bates and Sean Higgins
and Peter Frank, and how safe they all were. And
you'd know that life would never be safe with Corey
Haraden.*

"Hey," came a soft call from the driver's seat. A
gentle hand shook her knee. "Are you okay? I didn't
mean to upset you. You can do anything you want
while you're here. It's your choice."

Corinne's eyes flew to Corey's, revealing a momentary panic. *It's your choice.* That was precisely the
problem. For the first time in her life, Corinne half
wanted to walk on the beach by moonlight with an attractive man. But temptation was the root of all evil,
wasn't it?

"Cori?"

"I'm fine." She lowered her head and cleared her
throat, clutching her hands tightly in her lap. Slowly

and carefully she raised her eyes to the window. "I'm fine."

"Then do me a favor?" With his one free hand he gently pried open her fingers, then slid his thumb across their undersides.

"What?" she managed to breathe, but barely. She could feel it coming, something suggestive. How to act, how to answer...

"My sunglasses. They're in the glove compartment. Could you get them for me?"

She swallowed once. His sunglasses. "Sure," she said with an astounding amount of poise, given the brief hell she'd just been through. Within seconds she'd drawn out the sunglasses and handed them over.

"Thanks." He slipped them over the bridge of his nose and repositioned both hands on the wheel. "That's better. It was a little overcast when I was driving in, but the sun's pretty bright now. I wear lenses, so I'm sensitive to the glare."

"Lenses? As in *contacts*?"

"Hard to believe, I know. You were beginning to think I was perfect, and now I disillusion you by confessing to being myopic. Have I spoiled everything?"

He was teasing her, but she was thinking beyond that. "Why do you wear contacts?" She leaned forward to study the way the aviator glasses sat on his nose. "You look just fine with glasses." An understatement, but it would do.

"I'm vain. I admit it. I also see better with contacts, not to mention the fact," he added in a self-derogatory undertone, "that I don't have to scramble around looking for the glasses I've misplaced."

"I never would have guessed you were wearing contacts," she went on, still vaguely amazed.

"Y'mean, because I'm not squinting and blinking and tearing all over the place?" He chuckled. "I did that for a while and let me tell you, it was awful. I was a freshman in college at the time, and I was trying to impress everyone and everything in sight. I was just about to give up and walk around blind when things started getting better. Then I switched to soft lenses a while back, and it was a piece of cake."

Corinne narrowed an accusatory gaze on him. "So, that gorgeous green isn't yours at all. What color are your eyes?"

"Green."

"No, your *real* eyes."

"Green. My lenses are clear."

"Really?"

"Really."

"Oh." *Gorgeous green.... How could you, Corinne?* "I suppose you don't color your hair, either."

"Color my hair? Are you kidding? Hey, I may wear contacts so no one knows I'm nearsighted, but the rest of me is for real." He pinched his neck, then his arm, then his thigh. "Go ahead. Give it a try. No wood. No plastic."

"I'll take your word for it," she conceded quickly.

"Not that my hair was always this color. Right through my teens, it was bright red. Hence, the name."

"Name?"

The glance he darted her told him that she had no idea what he was talking about. "Uh, never mind that," he said under his breath.

"What name?"

"It's not important."

"If it's not, what's the harm in telling me?"

"Why are you curious all of a sudden?"

"Because you put the bug in my ear. What were you called?"

He shifted in his seat and mumbled, "I thought Alan would have mentioned it. He's always bringing it up."

"Corey..."

He sighed. "The Cardinal. It's a relic of my past. Let's leave it there."

Something happened then that made Corey's discomfort worth itself ten times over. Corinne laughed. It wasn't a boisterous laugh, actually wasn't much more than a step above a chuckle, but it was a laugh and it was genuine.

"The Cardinal? That's terrific. I assume it doesn't refer to the religious type?"

"Not quite," he said, but he shot one glance after another her way. "Do you know that's the first time I've seen you smile, much less laugh?"

The laugh was a memory, and the smile faded. "I do it from time to time." She wasn't sure why she'd done it this time, but assumed it had something to do with learning that Corey was fallible. He didn't have twenty-twenty vision, and he'd had bright red hair that had earned him the nickname the Cardinal. Not that there was anything intrinsically amusing about myopia, or overwhelmingly comical about red hair, or hysterically funny about a nickname, but they were all so personal, and he was definitely sheepish about the last, and there'd been something boyish about him just then that had...made her laugh.

"You should laugh more often," he said. "It's a lovely sound."

"I'm sure." She turned her head back to the window.

"Oh, boy, here we go again," he muttered, then raised his voice. "There's nothing wrong with laughing, Cori. Even if it is at my expense."

"You have to admit that a name like the Cardinal is a little ridiculous."

"I admit it, I admit it." He paused. "Granted, it's had its moments...."

"Like when?"

"Like when everyone had nicknames, only mine was a little more regal than the others. You have to agree that it's regal."

She didn't want to answer that one, so she slid him a skeptical gaze. "You don't look like a redhead. Your skin tans too well."

"Someone way back on my mother's side had red hair. I inherited it. That's all."

Corinne returned her eyes to the road. "I know a man who's called the Silver Fox," she said quietly. "He originally got the name because he had a full head of gray hair by the time he was thirty. He's forty-eight now, but the name has stuck even though many of his friends have gone gray, too. And the reason the name has stuck is that not only is he silver, but he's a fox. Quick and sly, darting in and out, taking what he wants then scampering away." She looked at Corey. "Aside from your hair, why did they call you the Cardinal?"

"My hair. That was it." He stuck out his chin and flexed his neck. "Well, after the fact they said it was because I flew around a lot."

"Euphemistically."

"Yeah. Hell, Cori, I've already told you that. I never claimed to be a saint."

"Do tell."

Corey grunted but said nothing more. He was furious at himself for having mentioned the name, because it advertised a side of him that he'd just as soon have kept from her. On the other hand, she'd laughed. She'd actually laughed. Which either meant that she thought he was a jerk or that he'd managed to lower her guard just enough to allow a ray of the sunlight she had inside to seep through.

He kind of liked that last idea. He didn't find her sunlight glaring.

Nor, he realized the more he thought about it, was he ashamed of his past. He couldn't hide what he'd been; he shouldn't have to. But he certainly could show Corinne that he'd grown up a bit. If she could learn to appreciate what he was now, she'd be able to accept his past.

What he needed, he decided as he directed the car across the double set of bridges leading to Hilton Head, was a happy compromise. A little mischief, a little propriety. He could live with that. And she wouldn't be able to resist it.

# 4

Hilton Head Island was shaped like a foot. At the ankle were plantations with such picturesque names as Rose Hill, Moss Creek and Indigo Run. At the heel was Port Royal, along the sole, Palmetto Dunes, Long Cove and Shipyard. Sea Pines, as Corey had informed Corinne, encompassed the toe. Shortly before they entered it, they stopped for lunch.

Ruby Tuesday had a cosmopolitan casualness to it. Stained glass abounded, as did overhanging Tiffany lamps. The tables were gaily set, the menu diverse and attractive. Though Corinne half suspected that the lift in her spirits was due to sheer relief at having left the intimate confines of Corey's car, she couldn't have picked a more jaunty place in which to enjoy that relief.

Fully intending to avail herself of the salad bar they'd passed on the way to their table, she ordered a quiche to Corey's baconburger. When he added fried zucchini sticks and potato skins to the order, she raised a brow.

"They're super here," he assured her. "You'll see."

She thought it best not to argue. Her stomach had settled once they'd hit the island, and as they'd cruised onward over Route 278 with Corey pointing out the sights, she'd allowed herself to ease up a bit. Being in a public restaurant helped. If the rest of the trip was going to be people oriented, she might actually survive.

While they waited for their drinks, Corey told her more about Hilton Head in general and, in specific, how he'd come to settle on the island. The discussion was impersonal, as far as her own involvement went, and for the briefest of illusionary moments, she could pretend that he was just another client filling her in on his background.

Then the moment was over, the illusion gone, and Corinne knew that she'd never worked with a client quite like Corey. When they stood to make their way to the salad bar, she was abruptly reminded of how heart-stoppingly tall and lithe limbed he was. When he paused several times along the way to greet friends who'd waved, she saw that he was well-known, well liked and well schooled in the art of trading light-hearted quips. When he plucked a black olive from the salad bar and popped it directly into his mouth, then sent her a shrug and a sheepish half grin, she sensed a charming naughtiness to him. And when he winked at the waitress who brought their meal, she knew for sure that he was a killer.

"So. Tell me about some of the other projects you've handled," he said after he'd taken the first large bite of his burger.

Having taken several deep, if surreptitious yoga-type breaths that had brought her pulse back to normal, Corinne was willing to indulge him. Work was safe ground. "I've done some interesting things in the past few months. One was a project for a university that wanted to know how its alumni felt about different issues."

''The alumni being the money givers, hence important.''

She nodded. ''Then there was a survey for a nationwide sporting goods manufacturer who wanted to know why people weren't buying his tennis rackets. We did a mail-out using customer lists from outlets the manufacturer supplied, as well as membership lists from tennis clubs.''

''They give out lists?''

''Not willingly. We had to sweeten the offer by promising the clubs free rackets for their staff. Some of them turned us down outright, which didn't say a lot for the racket.''

Corey saw it, that glimmer of dry amusement in her eyes, and though it never reached her lips, he felt buoyed. ''What else?'' he asked, reaching blindly for a zucchini stick.

''Projects?'' It wasn't fair that a man should have eyes like his. Green as emeralds, capable of cutting, probing, exciting. She wanted to think that she was immune to the last, but the tiny ripples dancing in her chest told her differently.

Projects. Concentrate, Corinne. Projects. ''They've been varied, more so than I thought when I first went to work for Alan.''

''Why did you? Go to work for Alan, that is.''

''He offered me a job in the field I wanted.''

''You've always lived in Baltimore?''

''Yes.''

''Went to college there, too?''

''Goucher.''

He grinned as he munched on another zucchini stick, and his gaze slanted off into memory. ''I once knew a girl at Goucher. She was the sister of one of my fraternity brothers. Really pretty girl." One eye closed as he calculated the time frame. "No, she'd have graduated at least five or six years before you. You wouldn't have known her." He focused full-force on Corinne again. "I'm sorry I interrupted. Go on."

She'd been distracted by that single eye that had closed. It had been an adorable gesture, impulsive and unpretentious. But the worst of it was that it had disarmed her so, that when both eyes had connected with her again she'd been unprepared for their force. Were green eyes always as magnetic? She didn't think she'd ever known anyone with green eyes before; if she had, she didn't remember. For that matter, she didn't remember what it was Corey had supposedly interrupted.

"You'll have to ask another question," she said as calmly as she could.

"Did you stay in Baltimore because of your grandmother?"

"I thought you wanted to know about my work."

"I do. In time. Right now, I want to know about your grandmother." He punctuated the declaration with another bite of his burger.

Corinne took the opportunity of his mouth being full to go off in the direction she preferred. "Alan is a remarkable business-getter. He's attracted clients ranging from banks to utilities to shoe manufacturers to politicians."

Unfortunately, Corey's mouth was empty again. "Julie said you have a sister. Where does she live?"

"New York City. We do a lot of work there. Several months ago, I did a survey for a publishing house on Sixth Avenue."

"Why would a publishing house in Manhattan go to Baltimore for market researchers? Aren't there plenty right in the city?"

"Yes, but Alan happened to have impressed one of the vice presidents of this particular house, so we got the contract."

"Does your sister have any kids?"

"One."

"Sex?"

"Obviously."

His lids lowered, then rose, and he sighed. "Of the child, of the child. Is it a boy or a girl, Cori?"

She was as straight-faced and poised as ever. "A boy, Corey."

"Cute?"

"Very."

"You're not eating."

"I'm talking. I can't eat while I talk."

He should have known that. While he had no qualms talking around a French fry or a pickle on occasion, he doubted Corinne would think of doing it. "Okay. Eat now. We'll talk later."

Corinne picked up her fork and ate some of the quiche, but Corey's eyes touched her like sticky fingers, making her want to wiggle. Since she couldn't do that, she set down her fork and began to talk again.

"The nice thing about market research is that it never goes out of style. In fact, business is better when everything else goes out of style. Take clothing. Merchandisers are forever wondering what people will want to buy next season, or the next."

"I thought London or Paris or Milan determined that."

She shook her head. "Haute couture has a limited following. The majority of American buyers don't care what's being shown in Paris or Milan, because those clothes are impractical for everyday life, not to mention out of sight price-wise. We're talking about the average American, who needs reasonably priced and sensible clothes to wear to work or school, or to a movie or a party at a friend's."

"Are you saying that the American public is stylishly ignorant?"

*Cute, Corey, cute.* "Not at all. But the American public knows, in general, what it wants. And what it wants may or may not be a copy of a Dior original. That's where we come in. We canvass cross-sections of the population, asking what they like to wear, what they don't, how much they'll spend. Fads come and go. Tastes change. I'd be wrong if I said that the public isn't influenced by what *Vogue* or *GQ* or *Seventeen* are showing, but only to an extent. Americans are freethinkers. They'll go along with a trend or modify it if they like it, but if they don't, it isn't worth the manufacturers' time or money to try to force it down their throats."

"So you tell the manufacturers what to produce."

"We tell them what the buying public tells us. They have to make their own decisions from there. Actually, I think our work is even more useful when it comes to chain stores. Something like The Limited will merchandise differently in New York than it will in Boston or Baltimore. The Midwest will stock differently from the East, and the West Coast is in a class by itself."

Corey grinned, and there was a conspiratory hush to his voice. "I bet you get lots of inside information about what's going to be hot and what's not. That's valuable stuff. You can be on the forefront of American fashion."

"Not quite," she said, well aware that her slacks and blouse were a far cry from the brighter, more sporty and daring outfits worn by other women in the restaurant. "I dress in a way that suits my personality."

"Ve-ry ti-dy," he teased, then held up a hand. "Not that I'm complaining, mind you. It's kind of nice to be with a woman who isn't hanging out every which way." He shut his eyes in immediate self-disgust. "Thank you, Corey. That was lovely."

"At least it was honest," she returned with a shrug. "If women who hang out every which way turn you on, that's great."

"They don't turn me on. Well, maybe they have sometimes, but I'm getting a little beyond that."

"Beyond being turned on?"

"Beyond things that, uh, that hang out for everyone to see. I guess I'm getting private in my old age. Or maybe possessive is the right word. Better still, make that conservative."

"Ahhh. Conservative." Her gaze dropped to his oversize top, which may have been fashionable and was far from avant-garde but could hardly have been called conservative. "That makes sense."

"You don't like this?" he asked, tucking in his chin and studying the pale purple pullover. "I thought it was kinda nice. A little different, but not too much." He raised surprisingly unsure eyes to Corinne.

"Go on," she coaxed, teasing him without realizing quite what she was doing. "I'm enjoying this. I've always wondered what goes through a man's mind when he's buying clothes or picking something from his closet.''

"A lot." Particularly when he wanted to impress someone, as Corey had wanted to do today. It had taken him half an hour to decide what to wear. He'd considered a blazer and slacks but ruled them out as being too stuffy for the setting. He'd considered a shirt and jeans, but vetoed them as being too hot. He'd considered shorts, but his legs would have shown, and while he had no argument with his legs, he feared Corinne wasn't ready for them yet.

"Is there a color you think looks best on you?" she was asking.

That was easy. "Green or blue. Or pale purple."

"A style?"

He smirked. "Dashing."

She paused. "Do you look at yourself in the mirror?"

"Of course."

"And push things around a little?"

"Sure."

One brow went up. "How about turning around and looking over your shoulder to see if your pants are too tight?"

"They never are. I don't carry weight there."

"You don't seem to carry weight anywhere," she blurted out, "but you're big. Where does it go?"

For a woman who projected such an air of indifference, she was remarkably observant, he mused. He'd gone from interviewer to interviewee in several short minutes, and he couldn't have been happier. It showed in his grin. "Height, woman. And muscle. Solid muscle."

"Do you work out?"

"I live. That's enough of a workout."

She nodded. "A manual laborer. I see."

"I've never had any complaints about my hand work," he drawled, then caught himself. Double entendres, particularly those with sexual overtones, rolled off his tongue far too easily. He'd have to watch it.

"I'm sure you haven't," she drawled right back, surprising him, confusing him, pleasing him....

He cleared his throat, then reached for the potato skins. "Here. You haven't had any of these." He deftly slid one onto her plate. "Go ahead. Tell me what you think."

She studied the offering. "I think I'm full."

"You don't like the way it looks?" he asked in dismay.

"I *love* the way it looks, but I've had enough to eat."

"Take a bite," he ordered.

Her eyes met his. "Why?"

"Because I said so."

"Not good enough."

"You'll like the way it tastes. They do something here with Cheddar cheese and bacon bits. I'm telling you, these skins are unique."

"Maybe another time."

"Now."

"Corey..."

"You don't have to worry about gaining weight. Besides, the skin of the potato has all the vitamins. You may not be able to see them, but they're in there, all those little goodies."

She stared at him.

He waggled a finger from the potato skin toward her mouth.

She didn't budge.

"Am I the boss on this job?" he asked.

"When we're working, yes."

"And you said that the only time you wouldn't be working was when you were alone in your room at night."

"You said I could take three meals, plus coffee breaks."

"I've changed my mind. So—" he took a breath "—Cardinal Rule Number One. Never argue with the boss." He tossed his chin toward the potato skin. "Eat."

"I thought you wanted me to forget that name."

"I've changed my mind."

"I thought you said that I could do whatever I wanted while I was here."

"Changed my mind about that, too."

"Then I have no choice?"

"Nope."

To his astonishment, she proceeded to cut a small piece of the skin and eat it. After the fact, she was equally astonished, but it had nothing to do with the luscious taste in her mouth and everything to do with the fact that she'd obeyed his command. No, that was wrong, she assured herself. She hadn't really obeyed him, because he hadn't really commanded. They'd been bantering, and she'd enjoyed it. Why else would she have let it drag on so long? Why else would she have given in and sampled what he'd been pushing?

But then, there was no harm done. He was right. She didn't have to worry about gaining weight.

Over the next two days she began to wonder whether she'd been premature in that assessment. It seemed that much of her research was done over a meal, and none of them were in any way, shape or form reminiscent of the instant hot cereal breakfasts or yogurt and apple lunches or chicken-salad-to-go dinners she too often wolfed down in Baltimore. Moreover, each meal-meeting was held at a different hotel or restaurant, in keeping with Corey's wish that she sample as much of the island as possible.

At dinner Wednesday night she talked with the owners of two of the other hotels. Over breakfast Thursday she met with a group of shopkeepers, over lunch with half a dozen restauranteurs, over dinner with a trio that owned a seeking-to-expand condominium complex. Friday's breakfast saw additional shopkeepers, lunch another pair of hoteliers, dinner a group of sportsmen specializing in boat charters. Not all of the people with whom she spoke were direct investors in the project, but every one had a personal stake in the island.

Aside from the quantity of food she consumed, several things amazed Corinne. First, she amassed an incredible amount of information about Hilton Head and its offerings. Second, beyond initial introductions for which he was always present, she saw little of Corey. Third, she was almost sorry about that.

Corey Haraden brought a certain sparkle with him wherever he went. At the start, he'd made her nervous, but, as time passed, that nervousness mellowed. When he was present, she felt challenged, on her toes, strangely alive, and even after he'd gone, a sense of anticipation remained.

Professionally, she wanted to please him. He'd hired her; she had to justify that action. Throughout each and every meeting he'd arranged she was at her confident, intelligent, inquisitive best, and that gave her a sense of inner satisfaction such as she hadn't felt before.

She liked Corey, she realized as she lay in bed late Friday night. She hadn't wanted to, but she did. He was generous; one glance around the plush executive suite he'd insisted she use was testimony to that. He was effective; every person he'd contacted had shown up to meet her, some with more open minds than others but all with style. He was considerate; when he felt a meeting had gone on long enough, he showed up to take her away for a break—a sight-seeing drive, or a walk through one local spot or another en route to the next meeting. He was well behaved; aside from the occasional outrageous remark to one of his fellow entrepreneurs, he conducted himself in a thoroughly businesslike manner.

He didn't touch her. He didn't push her. He didn't suggest that they go dancing or for midnight walks on the beach. All of which told her that he'd finally accepted what she'd known all along: they were very different types, and different types they would always be.

Still, she liked him. That was okay and safe and acceptable. She decided that she could like him without feeling threatened, which was why, when he phoned her room early on Saturday morning and told her to prepare for a half day of fun before he took her to the airport that afternoon, she readily accepted his invitation.

She had second thoughts the minute she opened the door. Corey was wearing a pair of shorts and a three-button T-shirt that hugged the muscles of his chest. It hugged the muscles of her chest, too, or she felt that it did, because she was suddenly having trouble breathing. He was gorgeous...that chest...those legs... She swallowed hard, then tore her eyes from him and grimaced down at her own clothes. She wore the same slacks and blouse she'd worn three days before for the trip south. She'd thought they were sporty—she'd been wearing skirts and blouses or dresses for the meetings—but now she felt strangely...dowdy.

"I'm sorry," she murmured, fluttering an uncharacteristically vague hand toward her outfit. "I didn't bring anything more casual."

Corey wasn't about to let her feel uncomfortable for long. "No shorts? No problem. We can remedy that. Come on." Before she could open her mouth again, he'd slipped his elbow through hers and was sweeping her toward the elevator.

She'd found her tongue by the time they reached his car. "It's really okay," she said quickly. She envisioned him dragging her into a store and making her try on one indecent outfit after another. She'd *die*. "I'll be flying out at four. This way I won't have to bother to change."

"You'll have time to change if you want, but you don't have to," he commented as they drove off. "People wear everything on planes nowadays. You'll be more comfortable in something freer."

"I'm comfortable now." *Lie, Corinne, lie. You're about as comfortable as a German shepherd in an airline doggy box.*

"You've worked for two and a half days straight. You deserve a break."

"I'll have a break tonight and tomorrow."

"Today. That was the deal. Today we're going to relax."

His voice was as firm as the rest of him. Firm, sturdy, well toned, devastating. It wasn't fair! "Where are we going?"

"First, to a little store in Harbortown. Look on it as research, if you want. You haven't done any shopping here, yet many guests on the island spend hours at it. Don't you want to know what they find?"

"I'm not a good shopper," she said to the window. "I go once each season, buy everything I need, then avoid stores like the plague."

"Maybe you haven't been in the right stores with the right people," he ventured, but where she'd have expected a leer there was pure innocence. "It won't take us long. I know what I want."

"Corey, what I'm wearing is just *fine*."

He shot her a glance. "Then we're headed in the right direction, anyway. I'll stop at home and change. If you insist on wearing that, I'll put on a shirt and slacks."

Corinne knew that he could put on heavy work boots, thick wool pants, a turtleneck, sweater and jacket and she wouldn't feel any safer. Had she really thought she could like him without being threatened? Her nervousness had returned in full—so much for mellowing—but who wouldn't be nervous with a body like Corey's no more than inches away? His shoulders were sturdy beneath his T-shirt, his bare arms leanly corded. His legs were long and bronzed, thighs matted with dark hair, calves slightly smoother, ankles knobby in a thoroughly masculine way.

He was the one who was scantily dressed, so why was she the one who felt totally exposed?

Corey slid a glance to his side-view mirror, pulling to the right in response to a passing car. "I guess I ought to warn you that we're going sailing. I thought you'd like to see the island from Calibogue Sound. The breeze is good, but the sun's hot. If you make me change, I'll broil."

Her lips thinned. "Thank you. Now I feel like a heel."

"No, no. It's okay. If you want, I'll change."

"No, no. It's okay. Don't bother."

"I can. It's no trouble."

Maybe it wouldn't be trouble for him, Corinne mused, but she didn't relish the idea herself. She wasn't sure if she was up to seeing his house. She wasn't sure if she was up to being there while he changed. He'd take off his clothes. True, she'd be in another room, but just thinking about it was debilitating. Something was wrong with her. She'd never been this way. Maybe she was suffering heat prostration. That was it, she decided, ignoring the fact that she'd spent ninety percent of the past two and a half days in air-conditioned environments. Heat prostration. Definitely.

"I said, it's okay," she murmured weakly.

"Are you sure?"

"Yes."

"We'll go shopping?"

"*Yes.*"

"Atta girl," he crooned with a smile.

His smile lingered through the rest of the drive, broadening when he drove her through the oak-and-moss tunnel he'd told her about, then relaxing back into a self-satisfied grin when they arrived in Harbortown, parked and made their way to the store he had in mind. He was grinning when he tugged a matching shorts and tank top set from a shelf and wasn't daunted when she shook her head. He was grinning when he pointed to a chic tennis-type ensemble, fully expecting her to veto that, too, which she did. What he wasn't prepared for was her eye catching on a perky T-shirt dress. It was scoop-necked and short-sleeved, and the drop waist was broadly elasticized.

She looked at it, turned to another shelf, looked at it again, turned away, then came back. She'd never bought anything like it and didn't know why she was considering it now. It was a little too sporty, a little too chic, but there was something about the softness of the fabric and its deep blue color and the silk-screened design on the front depicting a horizon of pink and gray clouds that appealed to her.

"I like it," came the deep voice by her ear. "Take it."

"I . . . don't know . . . I'd have to try it on."

"Then try it on. Hurry. I'm hungry."

The look she tossed over her shoulder was quelling.

"Breakfast," he explained. "I haven't had a thing to eat today. Quick. Try on the dress."

"It's not a dress. It's a . . . a . . ."

"Dress. Go on." He tossed his head toward a changing room. "Give it a try."

She lifted the dress from the rack and studied it a minute longer. When she felt Corey's hand nudging her onward, she went.

Quickly stripping off her clothes—between nervous glances at the door through which she half expected Corey's emerald eyes to bore—she drew the fabric over her head and shimmied it down her body. Then she looked in the mirror and slowly, helplessly, smiled.

The dress was adorable. The neckline generously framed her throat, the sleeves fell loose to her elbow and were ripe for rolling, and the elasticized waist pushed the fabric up to create an overblouse effect.

There were, she decided, only two minor problems. The first was the length; the hem fell short of her knees by two inches. She'd never in her life worn a miniskirt, hadn't even *considered* it. Still, she had the legs, and she'd shaved them just last night....

The second problem was the neckline. As she shifted the fabric here, then there, she found that it was a little *too* generous. When she pulled one shoulder up to cover her bra strap, the other fell to expose not only the strap but her shoulder. It was possible, she debated as she tugged both sides at once, to cover both straps, but would they stay covered?

"Cori?"

She spun around. He had to be leaning against the door, with his voice slithering through the crack. She clutched the fabric to either side of her neck. "Yes?"

"C'mon out. Let me see."

"It looks pretty good."

"Let me see."

"Maybe I ought to try the shorts and tank top, after all."

"Let me see the dress."

Taking a deep breath, she relaxed her hold on the neckline and hesitantly opened the door.

Corey was the one to take a deep breath then. Corinne looked twenty years old, fresh and innocent. Her throat was smooth, her skin an ivory coverlet over the graceful line of her collarbone. Her arms were fine boned, her legs slender but feminine. Contrary to his original belief, there was nothing skinny and boyish about her. There was a fragility, yes, but it appealed to him. Barefoot, she was waiflike. She made him feel taller, stronger and protective.

He let out his breath in an appreciative, if slightly shaky, whoosh. "Take it."

She scrunched up her face. "Isn't it a little . . . a little . . . loose?"

"That's how it's supposed to be. It's supposed to feel free and easy. You can't get free and easy with tight. Loose is the style. It looks great!"

Unsure still, Corinne turned to face the mirror. "I should take it?"

"Definitely."

"It's not *too* free and easy?"

"Not in my eyes, but my eyes aren't yours, and you're the one who'll be doing the wearing. Do you like it?"

She took a last look. One of the shoulders had begun to slip. There was something daring about that added patch of skin that should have shocked her, but didn't. "Yes. I like it." Of course, on the opposite side of that patch of skin was a strap that was inching its way to center stage.

Corey, who'd been looking over her head at her reflection in the mirror, leaned down to her ear. "Take off the bra. It won't hurt."

Her eyes flew to his.

"No one will see," he coaxed in that same private whisper.

"You will," she croaked.

"I won't be looking. I'll be tending the sails." He straightened. "What size shoe do you wear?"

"Six double A."

"I'll see if they have a pair of sneakers." Turning, he started off, closing the dressing room door behind him.

She was gnawing on her lower lip, still trying to decide what to do a minute later, when his voice came again. "Open up, Cori. I have sneakers and a bag. Put your other clothes inside and we can take off."

*Take off.* The dilemma, in a nutshell. She opened a wedge in the door and accepted the sneakers and bag, then promptly dropped them on the floor and turned back to the mirror.

Should she, or shouldn't she? She'd never done it before. Would she jiggle? But she was pretty small, and if she did say so herself, pretty firm. Would anything show? The dress was dark in color, and the fabric was sturdy enough. Soft, but sturdy. Safe?

"Are you ready?" came the voice from the crack.

"Almost," she breathed quickly.

*Go ahead. Take it off.*

I shouldn't.

*Would you rather worry about the straps all day?*

At least I'd be covered.

*You'll be covered anyway, so what are you afraid of?*

He'll take it as an invitation.

*He'll be busy with the sails.*

That's what he said, but I don't trust him.

*You don't trust him, or you don't trust you?*

Good point.

*So where does that leave us?*

"Cori? Are you still there?"

"Be right out," she gasped. With a despairing look at herself in the mirror, she pushed aside the shoulders of the dress, unhooked her bra, tugged the dress into place, balled the bra and stuck it in the middle of her other clothes, all of which she crammed into the bag without thought to the dry-cleaning bill she was buying.

As she knelt to put on the sneakers, she tried to rationalize what she would normally have classified as insane. She was on vacation—well, for the day, at least. And she'd earned a little freedom. This wasn't Baltimore; this was Hilton Head Island. One was more formal, one more relaxed. Okay, so she was feeling a little removed from reality, but would it really do any harm? What could possibly happen during a half-day sail, with Corey at the helm all the time? She wouldn't be shocking him; he'd suggested it himself. If there was any problem, *he'd* be the one at fault.

"Corey to Cori. Come in, Cori."

Snatching the bag on her way to her feet, she opened the door and hurried past him. "Do you have scissors I could use to cut off the tags?" she asked the girl at the cash register.

Corey backed slowly toward the front door of the shop. She'd done it. Bless her, she'd done it. And heaven help him, he liked it. He liked it too much. The problem was going to be keeping his hands off her—

He bumped into someone, twirled around with an apology slipping from his lips, only to find that the someone was a free-standing rack of bathing suits. Cursing softly, he hurried to the door and stepped into the sunshine. He'd already told the salesgirl to bill him for the dress and sneakers, and wondered if Corinne would make an issue of it. Maybe that would be good. If she did something to irritate him, he wouldn't feel so damned attracted to her.

To this day, he couldn't figure out the basis of the attraction. She was so different from the other women he'd known, but being attracted to her for the sake of variety only went so far. He'd seen her in action during the past few days, and though he'd tried to make himself scarce for her sake—he'd sensed she'd be more comfortable without his standing over her shoulder— he'd seen enough to tell him she was tops in her field. Alan had a bargain in her. Alan should lock her into a long-term contract. Alan should give her a raise.

But he could only spend so much time thinking of Alan.

Corinne puzzled him. With her straight back, her tipped-up chin and her ever-so-organized approach to life, she should be boring him, yet she wasn't. Her self-contained wall was a challenge. Just when he'd begin to despair of ever breaking it down, she'd toss a word or two his way with an inflection of humor, and he'd be off and running again. When he'd been asking about her sister, for instance.

*"Does she have any kids?"*

*"One."*

*"Sex?"*

*"Obviously."*

She'd offered it so dryly that he'd been momentarily stunned. It wasn't that he'd doubted she knew about the birds and the bees, but that he'd never have expected her to parry that way with him.

Other things puzzled him, such as why she hadn't
found a man to love, why she kept such a tight rein on
her emotions, why she thought she couldn't handle
him.

The last was really a joke. Little did she know, but
she'd been handling him since the first day he'd seen
her. He'd plotted and schemed, driven his secretary
wild with demands designed to free him up for another trip to Baltimore or three days here. He'd toned
down his flamboyancy, had agonized over what he'd
do with Corinne, what he'd say to her, had even
ousted a regular guest from the executive suite at the
hotel so that she could have it.

And she thought she couldn't handle him. Hah!

Not that he minded being handled, and that surprised him, too. He'd never been one to arrange his life
around a woman; that he was doing it now brought
him back to square one. What was it about Corinne
that tugged at him so? He supposed it could be her
independence. She had a mind of her own, which
she'd demonstrated by giving him five days' notice of
her arrival, rather than procrastinating for aeons as
he'd expected. He supposed it could be her dedication. She was loyal to Alan, and Corey was envious.
And then, he reflected, there was the soft side of her,
the vulnerable side that slipped through occasionally
and was quickly recovered. He recalled the time she'd
spoken of the Silver Fox. There'd been a distant look
in her eyes and a sadness in her voice that made him
wonder who the Silver Fox was and what he'd done to
Corinne to evoke that sadness.

"Corey?"

He turned to find her directly behind him, holding
herself with remarkable dignity given the bag she

hugged to her chest. That, too, charmed him. Shyness . . . self-consciousness . . . he couldn't quite put a name to it, but it had obviously come with her change of clothes, and it fascinated him.

"All set?" he asked huskily.

"Uh-huh."

Automatically he reached for the bag, then, not wanting to force the issue of whatever it was she was feeling, extended the gesture into a gallant sweep of his arm. "Lead on."

It wasn't far to the car and not much farther, relatively speaking, to the spot Corey had decided on for breakfast. Somewhere along the way, Corinne had thrown caution to the winds. The bag with her clothes lay in her lap.

"This is your house," she stated as they approached the end of the road. If the dead end hadn't been a giveaway, the house itself would have done the trick. Though Corey hadn't described its features, he'd spoken of a sense of serenity, of otherworldliness, and that was precisely what the property conveyed. Everything in sight was green and rich, the lushly canopied house itself a shade of brown not unlike the trunks of the trees. Large windows mirrored the verdant landscape, while the low-slung wings of the house melted into it.

Serenity, otherworldliness, beauty—a welcome counterpoint to the trepidation she felt.

"You've eaten out for every meal since you got here," Corey was reasoning. "I thought we'd grab this one in. It'll be faster, and then we can go for that sail. Besides," he added in a sheepish mumble, "I left the drinks here. We'd have had to stop by to pick them up anyway."

So much for taking the easy way out and buying clothes rather than coming here for him to change, Corinne mused. But what was done was done. It wasn't worth the effort of arguing.

"Okay." She sighed in resignation as she slid from the car. "Let's take a look."

The look was wonderful, but then, she'd guessed it would be even before she'd stepped a foot inside. Corey's house flowed. There was no better way of putting it. One room flowed into the next, one functionally designated area into the next. Casablanca fans flowed into stucco walls, which flowed into leather furniture, marble tables and polished wood floors.

"Whaddya think?" he asked.

"It's wonderful," she said, and meant it. "And spotless. Either you're a super cleaner or—"

"It's the 'or,' and her name is Jontelle. Monday through Friday she cleans up the mess. On weekends, I'm on my own. It's a challenge."

"It's good for the soul," was Corinne's comment. Turning, she headed for the kitchen she'd seen moments before. There was something too...too Corey about the house. She'd feel better if she was busy. "What are we eating?" she asked as she pulled open the refrigerator.

Nudging her gently aside, he began to draw several covered bowls from the shelves. "Waffles. Sound okay?"

"Sounds fine. I'm impressed."

"Don't be until you try them. They may not be super, but at least I've tried."

She could see that he had. The bowls turned out to contain, in turn, waffle batter, fresh sliced strawberries, the largest raspberries she'd ever seen and a mound of newly whipped cream. If he was a cook on top of everything else, she'd sit down and cry.

Corey was looking from one bowl to another as though he'd forgotten something. Straightening a finger, he swiveled back to the refrigerator and extracted a carafe of orange juice.

"What can I do?" She felt awkward. She was used to being the doer, the one in command. It wouldn't have been so bad to sit back and let someone else do the work for a change if the spacious kitchen hadn't suddenly seemed so close.

He dug into the utensil drawer and came up with a ladle. "The waffle iron is in the cabinet to the right of the sink. Can you reach it?"

"Sure." Kneeling easily, she reached into the cabinet and brought out the iron. She looked at it, then looked harder. "Corey?" she asked quietly. "What's on the iron?"

He angled over and stared, before muttering a soft, "Oh, hell." Whipping away, he yanked open one of the upper cabinets, took out a plate, then another, looking at each in turn and with growing disgust. He set the plates on the counter with a clatter, snatched out a decidedly dirty glass and stared at it in dismay. Then he hung his head. "I can't believe I did that." Dropping his head back now, he eyed the ceiling. "I must have forgotten to run the dishwasher. I was in such a rush to get everything put away and neat, that I guess I didn't notice." With a sigh he brought his gaze down to hers. "That was bright."

"You put the waffle iron in the dishwasher?"

"Wasn't I supposed to?"

"No."

"Why not?"

"It ruins the electrical components."

"Oh." He thought for a minute, then his expression brightened. "I knew there was a reason I didn't turn the dishwasher on." Which didn't explain why last night's soiled dishes, glasses and cups were in the cabinet, but that was beside the point.

Corinne was the one to eye the ceiling then, but when another thought struck, she returned her gaze to Corey. "Has this thing gone through the dishwasher before?"

"No."

"Thank goodness. Jontelle must know enough to wash it by hand."

"I don't know. I'll have to remember to tell her."

"She hasn't washed it before?"

"It's new."

"Then ... you had waffles for dinner last night?"

"Of course not."

Corinne eyed the waffle iron. No doubt about it. It had been used at least once. Maybe he'd borrowed it from a friend? Puzzled, she lifted her gaze to Corey, only to find a flood of red on his cheeks.

The words shot from his mouth. "I bought it yesterday, thinking that I'd make us a terrific breakfast, but I'm not a breakfast person when I'm alone, and I've never made a waffle in my life, so I spent a while last night experimenting." He sighed. "I've always loved waffles."

Unable to help herself, Corinne burst out laughing. He was precious. Male through and through, but such a little boy at heart. He was looking so guilty, and so sheepish, and so disappointed in himself. How could you deal with a man who was lovable and deadly in the same breath?

You couldn't. At least, *she* couldn't.

*Do something, Corinne. Busy yourself somehow, so you don't have to think about him.*

"No problem," she said, standing to deposit the waffle iron in the sink. "It'll wash up in no time." Particularly with the way she went at it. She flipped on the hot water, rummaged beneath the sink for detergent and a sponge, then set to work with the energy of three muscle-bound dishwashers at a grease joint. Not that she'd ever been to a grease joint, she mused, but she imagined the amount of washing there'd be. On the other hand, maybe there wouldn't. At a posh French restaurant, perhaps, where the management went from table to table at the start of the evening making sure that each piece of china was mirror smooth and clean, but not at a grease joint. Which was probably why she'd never gone in one.

"I think it's clean, Cori."

The softly teasing voice brought her back to the present with a start. She sighed. "So it is." After a final rinse she dried the iron, then handed it over to the chef, who proceeded—after diligently reloading the automatic dishwasher with everything that had supposedly been washed before—to serve up the most delicious waffles Corinne had ever tasted.

Was it the waffles themselves, she wondered? Or the whipped cream? Or the fresh fruit? Or the confectionery sugar or the fresh-squeezed orange juice or the rich Jamaican coffee? It had to be one of those, she decided. Corey, himself, couldn't possibly have infused her with the pleasant sense of satiation she felt.

The pleasure lingered through the cleanup, through the drive into Shelter Cove, through the boarding of the boat that was moored there, through the casting off and setting of the sails. In fact, the pleasure was such that Corinne found herself smiling at the sun, laughing at Corey's quips, dropping her head back into the breeze and thoroughly forgetting that she was, by her standards, in a state of undress.

Corey didn't forget. He couldn't take his eyes off her. Shielded by dark glasses, his gaze touched every inch of her, bringing a pleasure in the vicinity of his heart and a distinct pain a bit lower.

# 5

Corey's fantasies hadn't been far off the mark. There was a woman of passion beneath Corinne's prim and proper facade. She seemed to have been freed by the wind and the sun, or maybe it was the distance from shore that allowed her to set her inhibitions aside. Whatever the case might be, she was delightful.

They talked of inconsequential things, like sailing and vacations and swashbuckling movies, and she opened up as she'd never done before. Gone was her intense concentration and the way she had of weighing every word before she spoke. Her brown eyes were warm and dancing, her smile free and easy. And her laugh...

Her laugh was as musical as the sweet *whoit-whoit* of the cardinal itself.

Likewise gone was the utter control she held over her body and with it, increasingly, Corcy's own control. Rather than sitting with her legs pressed together or neatly crossed, she had one tucked beneath the other, which would have been fine had she been wearing shorts, but she wasn't. The brief glimpse of white silk he was given when the skirt of her dress blew made him ache to touch what only the breeze now did.

Her arms and hands were another awakening. He'd known they were graceful, but that grace had been understated by the calm poses she'd always maintained. Now she gestured freely, and he found an elegance to her that went beyond refinement, just as he found a lure in her slim, rounded shoulders, bared—one or the other, not both, and ever elusively—by the neckline of her dress as it shifted with her movements.

Her breasts, though, were the best and the worst. He'd been too clever for his own good when he'd suggested she discard her bra, or maybe he'd wanted to prove she had nothing in that department worth mention. No, he corrected himself baldly, he'd known she had something and he'd wanted to see what it was. Well, he'd seen, all right. He'd seen that she hadn't needed a bra to begin with, because the upthrust of her breasts was natural and pert. He'd seen the way the T-shirt fabric clung to enticing curves and valleys. And he'd seen, heaven help him, he'd seen her flesh. She couldn't have known it when she reached over to retrieve the can of Coke she'd set on the floorboards, but the neckline of her dress had gaped just enough to give him a view of unconfined beauty.

No, she couldn't have known it because surely, if she had, she'd have gasped and gone red in the face. But then, Corey caught himself, Corinne Fremont didn't gasp and go red in the face. She drew herself up, straightened her shoulders and leveled a gaze that was cool and composed.

But she wasn't looking prim and detached now, and that was the problem. She looked eminently touchable, and Corey wanted to touch every bit as badly as he wanted her to stay the way she was. Therein lay the ultimate dilemma. If he touched, would she stiffen? If he kissed, would she draw back into her compact and tidy shell? If he whispered what he wanted to whisper, would she slap him across the face?

Out of sheer fear he did nothing but adjust the sails and guide the steering wheel to accommodate the shifting of the winds and their own direction as, time running out, they headed toward the cove.

Something happened to that fear, though, when they were back in the harbor with the luff lines secured; it turned to desperation. Time *was* running out. Within hours Corinne would be on her way back to Baltimore, and her orderly life would disallow everything she'd been here as though this day had never been.

He didn't want that.

She was tidying up the galley, which had furnished chips and nuts and fruit and drinks during their sail, when he came up behind her.

"Cori?" His voice was deep, but quiet and hesitant.

She turned to meet eyes whose green was somehow different, darker and smoky, and a prickle of apprehension slid down her spine. "This has been wonderful," she said, forcing lightness not because she didn't mean the words, but because that look in his eyes made her jumpy.

The contrast between jumpiness and the tranquility she'd experienced was marked. It wasn't that she hadn't been aware of Corey for the past few hours, because she had. She'd seen the agility of his fingers as he'd worked the lines, the flex of his muscles as he'd maneuvered the sails. She'd seen the play of the wind in his hair, seen the mark of the sun in shadows of perspiration on his shirt, seen, endlessly, the stretch of his long, lean, bronzed legs. She'd seen all these things, but she'd been in control. She'd made a decision to enjoy herself, and she had.

Now she realized that the dark glasses he'd worn had been shielding her. When she couldn't see his eyes, she couldn't know his thoughts, and when she didn't know those, she could deny the crux of his identity. She could pretend that he was any man, without the threat of specifics.

But the glasses were gone now and with them all pretense. He was Corey, and he wanted her. Suddenly all the physical things she'd noticed about him were personal and near. No longer could she be objectively appreciative of his body, because her own was clamoring for something beyond thought.

"I should drive you to the airport," he said softly.

"Yes," she answered as softly.

He moved an inch closer. "I'm glad we took this time together."

She nodded, unable to speak in the face of his sheer and utter magnetism. She'd never known anything like it and was as intrigued by the magnetism itself as by the man.

"Cori..." His voice was more husky. He lifted his hand, held it by her cheek, then touched her skin. It was rosy, kissed by the sun, cooled by the wind and smooth as the endless sky. "Tell me to go back on deck. You don't want this."

"I don't want this," she breathed, but there was little conviction in the words, even less in her eyes, which had gone wide with wonder and anticipation and need.

"I'm not your type."

"I know."

"You're not mine."

"I know."

"Then why is it I want to kiss you so badly?"

"Maybe," she whispered, swallowing, "because that way you'll know for sure that there's nothing there."

His fingers had slid into her hair and were stroking the short and silky windblown layers. "Is that what you're thinking?"

"I'm afraid I'm not thinking."

He had to smile at that, a smile of equal parts sadness and affection. *I'm afraid I'm not thinking.* So correct. So Corinne. "If you're not thinking, I may take advantage of you."

At that moment Corinne didn't know who she was. She couldn't comprehend the trembling of her knees or the palpitations in her chest or the currents of desire creeping into her belly. She didn't recognize the wispy sound of her voice, and she certainly didn't identify with the words that were coming from her mouth. Probably because she was too engrossed in Corey's mouth. His lips were thin but mobile. Had she never noticed them before? Or had she simply been too taken with his other features to study them?

"If you're going to take advantage of me," she dashed off a broken whisper, "you'd better hurry. If you wait, I'll start thinking, and if I do that, I'll remember how much I don't want this."

"I'll hurry," he said, but he didn't. He couldn't. There was too much to sense and to savor, like the feel of her face when he brought his other hand to frame it, and the softness of her lips when he slid his thumbs across them, and the sweet lemony scent of her when he closed his eyes and pressed his nose to her brow.

Then his thumbs receded, and his mouth fell to her lips, and he tasted her for the very first time. She was a delicacy, sweet, not lemon but raspberry. Perhaps because it seemed he'd been waiting forever for her to come into season, he sampled her slowly. Her lips were ripe, smooth and full. He sucked them languorously, shaping them to his mouth, shifting them around to appreciate every nuance of their form. His breath was coming unevenly, but he paused for only the quickest of gasps before returning for more.

Corinne. Pure as the driven snow and enticing as hell. Though an inch separated their bodies, he could feel her trembling. But if she was frightened, she did nothing to pull away, not when he slid his hands over her shoulders to her back and drew her fully against him, not when he deepened the kiss by coaxing her mouth wider and introducing her to his tongue.

Her teeth were small and even, and the way they clung together spoke of her inexperience. They were the tiny seeds of the raspberry, a little abrasive to the touch but so much a part of the fruit itself that he loved them, as well. He explored them, teased them, and like the raspberry seeds, with savoring they melted away.

Corinne shuddered when his tongue slid into the depths of her mouth. Her arms were around his waist, her hands clutching bunchfuls of his T-shirt. She needed support, because her limbs had grown fluid, and Corey's firm body provided a semblance of stability. She didn't think about what she was doing as she pressed herself closer. What he was doing felt so good that she was incapable of thinking beyond the moment.

She trusted Corey. She didn't have to think about that, or debate it, but on some deep level, one she might deny in a saner time, she did trust him. She'd trusted him with her life when they'd been sailing, when he'd drawn in the sails and set the boat at a perilous heel. She'd braced herself, nearly standing, against the gunwale and felt the rush of waves on her feet and wind in her hair. She'd known that Corey would keep her safe, so she'd given herself up to the pleasure of the moment, just as she was doing now.

His tongue filled her mouth, sending a swelling sensation through the rest of her body. That spreading pressure was inflammatory, as was the gentle strength of his probing. Her initial passivity melted before the fire of curiosity, prompting her own lips into movement, her own tongue into exploration. She was tentative at first, but the sigh of pleasure that joined his tongue in her mouth was ample encouragement to venture on.

Then his tongue was gone, and he was whispering her name in a sound that was hoarse but sweet. "Ah, Cori..." Such a quick study, he mused, she followed his lead, then gave herself up to instinct. But he wanted more. His muscles quivered with the force of restraint. If he could think of her once more as skinny and boyish, the pain of his arousal would ease, but he couldn't think of her that way, because his hands were working over her shoulders, back and hips, and her breasts were crushed to his chest, and everything he touched and felt spelled woman.

Her eyes were closed. He kissed them in turn, not caring if she was shutting out reality in favor of blind sensation, just knowing that he'd take her any way she came. When he fastened his mouth to hers with a greater hunger, he found it returned. And while he feasted on that oral lushness, he drew his hands forward, spreading them over her shoulders, then her throat and chest until they reached, then circled, then fully cupped her breasts.

A tiny moan came from deep in her throat, part purr, part gasp, part sigh. The faint jolt that shook her body spoke of her surprise, but she didn't pull away. She seemed in momentary suspension, not even breathing for an instant until he began to knead her lightly. With another small moan, she curled her arms around his neck and buried her face against his throat.

A vague voice of reason, edging beyond the passionate daze in Corey's mind, told him that if she'd wanted him to stop touching, she'd have flattened herself against him. But she hadn't. Her head and hips were against him, but her back was slightly bowed to allow for his caress and the shallowness of her breathing was the only sound he heard.

"You're perfect," he whispered. His fingers slid over and around her breasts, tracing their shape, committing it to memory. When he felt her swell into his touch, he increased the pressure until he was the one who could no longer bear the waiting. Then, and only then, did he touch the pads of his thumbs to her nipples.

The sound she made was louder this time.

His thumbs flew away. "I hurt you."

Her fingers were clutching the hair at his nape. Her voice was breathless against his throat. "No...no. Not hurt..."

"Shock?"

"Right through me...hot...do it again...."

So he did it again with exquisite tenderness, and the pleasure he gleaned from the feel of those hard twin nubs was enhanced by the way she sucked in her breath and even more by the way she pressed her hips to his.

It was instinct. She was searching for satisfaction in the way God had intended when He'd created man and woman. Corey believed that Corinne may have found an innocent semblance of satisfaction in the friction of their bodies. But he wasn't innocent. He was fully erect, and his hips were far from immobile. The friction he felt was nothing more than a stopgap measure for the kind of satisfaction he sought.

"Cori?" He lifted her face to his. He knew that his voice sounded gruff and that the gruffness was spawned by need, but he had to get her attention, "Look at me, Cori." His fingers tightened. "Open your eyes. Please, sweetheart?"

Corinne had never been anyone's sweetheart, at least never in a situation where her heart was pounding and her insides were aflame and the coil in her belly was painfully tight. The foreignness of the endearment brought her lids up.

"Do you know what's happening?" he asked. His tone was kind, but there was an urgency to it.

"No," she admitted in a high voice.

He let out a breath, could have laughed, then cried, but his fingers tightened around her head, and he forced his eyes to clear. "I want you, Cori, and if we keep going like this, one thing's going to lead to another, and before either of us knows it, we'll be sprawled on the floor making love. I want that badly, but I'm not sure you do, and right now I don't think I'd trust myself to take off my shirt, much less think about my shorts. I only have so much self-control, and it's going fast. Just about anything now will push me past the point of no return. I want it, Cori. I want it, but do you?''

Her eyes were large. She gave a tiny shake of her head, a shake that, seconds later, was augmented a trifle roughly by his hands. He felt angry at himself that he'd stopped, angry that he was doing something he'd never done before in his life, angry that she didn't relieve his anger and his incredible frustration by telling him to go on.

But she was Corinne. He skimmed her hair, then each of her features. She was Corinne. When it happened with her, it had to be right.

"I want you." He ground his hips into hers. "Do you feel it?"

She nodded. The way her eyes widened at his movement told him that what he'd suspected was correct. Instinct had been driving her on, rather than conviction or affection or understanding and conscious consent.

He let out a second breath in as many minutes, and his grasp of her loosened. Closing his eyes, he slid his arms around her and drew her into a gentle embrace. "You try a man's mind, Corinne Fremont."

"I'm sorry," came her muffled reply, and she tried to pull away.

He tightened his hold. "No. Just another minute. Give me a chance to . . . let me come down . . . not cold turkey." That was only one of the reasons he couldn't let her go just yet. The other was that he feared what he'd find when he released her.

It was with that fear in mind that he started to talk. His voice was low and carried a lingering thickness, but that didn't matter, because his words were from the heart. "What just happened, Cori, was something we both needed. It was right and good, but you'll probably agonize over it anyway. I don't want you to do that. I don't want you to look up at me with fear in those brown eyes of yours, or with regret, or worse, disgust. I don't think I could bear that." His arms were still; only his fingers moved in the merest of soothing strokes on her back.

"If you decide you don't want this to happen again, I'll accept it," he went on, "but only if you tell me why. I'll need to know why. Because I think we have something special here. I know that I haven't ever felt anything like it before, and I know that I don't want it to end."

He took a shuddering breath. "I'm going to let you go now. I don't want you to say anything or do anything, except gather your things together and leave this boat with me. I'll drive you to the airport and put you on that plane, and when you get back to Baltimore you can say and do anything you want. It's just that..." He faltered. He'd never said things like this to a woman and the words felt strange, even if the feelings were real. "It's just that I want to remember today as being beautiful. I don't want anything to spoil those memories. Whether it's true or not, I'd like to think what we've done—and I don't mean only this—" he gave her a quick squeeze "—but everything we've done today—has meant as much to you as it has to me. I'm feeling a little vulnerable right now. I don't want to be rejected." He paused, shut his eyes tight, then opened them. "Okay? No fights, no words, no recriminations?"

Corinne nodded. She wasn't capable of fights or words or recriminations just then. She wondered if she was even capable of gathering her things together and leaving the boat. Her body felt like rubber, and it buzzed.

But she did it. Corey set her back, then headed for the deck. She followed him, gathered her things together, then walked by his side to the car. They made the drive to the airport in silence and exchanged only her shoulder bag and the faintest of smiles when her flight was called. Straightening her shoulders and tipping up her head, she walked through the door and away from him without looking back.

Two things struck her as the plane picked up speed on the runway, lifted off and climbed northward out of Savannah. The first was that she was grateful for Corey's request. Silence had been the solution to a problem she wasn't yet ready to face.

The second was that she was still wearing the dress she'd bought that morning.

She changed, of course. She went into the first ladies' room she could find when she landed in Baltimore and replaced the dress with a skirt and blouse from her suitcase. It was only nine o'clock. She'd be home by nine-thirty, and since her grandmother didn't go to bed until ten, she knew she'd have a welcoming committee of one waiting at the door.

And so she did. With a hug for Elizabeth, she set down her bag and flipped through the mail on her way into the kitchen. She poured herself a glass of orange juice, then sat down at the table.

Elizabeth sat, too. The warmth of the May night notwithstanding, she was wearing a velvet robe, neatly buttoned and sashed. Her salt-and-pepper hair was freshly washed and wound into a tidy French knot at the back of her head, and her hands lay lightly in her lap. She was the image of regality.

"I see you got some sun," she observed pleasantly. Never one to use her tone of voice as a vehicle of opinion, she left that job to her eyes, which was why Corinne didn't look up from her sorting of the mail. She already knew her grandmother's opinion about the deleterious effect of sun on skin.

"Mmm-hmm. The weather was nice. How has everything been here, Gram?"

"Just fine. I had book club on Thursday and garden club yesterday. The toilet upstairs began to run, so I had the plumber in this morning."

"He fixed it, I assume," Corinne said, trying not to smile. Poor Elizabeth. Dripping faucets, running toilets and sticking doorbells were the bane of her existence. They seemed symbolic of the onset of decline, and decline, whether physical or emotional, was one thing Elizabeth could not abide. Nor could she abide sloppiness, tardiness or impoliteness, and the decadence of frivolity and spontaneity went without saying. She had her daily life scheduled with activities designed to make her a better person. Self-improvement was of prime importance on her agenda, and, hence, on the agenda she'd drawn up for her granddaughter's life. It was in the spirit of self-improvement that she accepted Corinne's work.

"Did you accomplish all you'd hoped to in South Carolina?" she asked along that vein.

"Uh-huh. I spent most of the time talking with people from the island. They were helpful. I think it'll be an interesting project." Interesting was one word for it. She didn't want to think of the other words just yet.

Rising from the table, she took a knife from the drawer and slit open a letter from her sister.

"That's the third letter you've received from Roxanne in the last month. Why has she started writing when she calls once a week?"

"I think she likes the exercise of writing." And the time it takes, Corinne mused, and the emotional outlet. Roxanne was as troubled as ever.

"That's a novel thought," Elizabeth said, oblivious to the pun. "She never cared for it when she was in school. I'm glad to see that she's finally awoken to its merits. I've always believed letter writing to be far superior to phoning. As you pointed out, it is an exercise. It's a mental challenge to express oneself well, when the recipient of one's efforts has nothing but the words on the page to go by. If the challenge is met, one can do so much more with the written word than the spoken word, not to mention the cost of long-distance phoning. It's a shame that Roxanne is in New York, rather than here."

"New York is where Frank is," Corinne pointed out. "He was established there long before Roxanne met and married him. Besides," she chided, "it's not that far. You could fly up to meet her for lunch any time you wanted."

"No. Flying makes me nervous. I've read articles about the problem of alcoholism among airline pilots. I don't think I'd trust them to get me there in one piece."

"Millions of people do it, Gram."

"Thank you, but I'll stay here. If Roxanne wants, she can fly down and meet me for lunch here."

Corinne did look at her grandmother then. Though Elizabeth had spoken in the same pleasant tone of voice, there was a hurt in her eyes that Corinne had known she'd find. This wasn't the first time they'd discussed Roxanne's visiting, and each discussion opened the same wound.

"It's not that she doesn't want to, Gram," Corinne tried to soothe, but it entailed a twist of the truth. "She's busy with Jeffrey, and Frank is always taking her to one business affair or another."

"I wish it were as simple as that, but you know as well as I do that Roxanne and I never got along. If it hadn't been for you acting as referee, we'd have been at each other's throats."

Corinne laughed. "You? At someone's throat? You're too much of a lady for that, Gram."

"I was speaking figuratively," Elizabeth went on calmly. "Roxanne has too much of her mother in her. I did my best to tame Cerise, but I failed. At least Roxanne is married to a stable man, but right up to the day of her wedding, I half expected her to bolt. I must say that I don't envy Frank his job, and I am not referring to business."

Corinne knew what her grandmother was saying, but there was another side of the problem that the older woman couldn't know, not having read Roxanne's letters. Roxanne appeared to feel that Frank was incapable of separating the roles of businessman and husband, and Corinne couldn't help but fear that there might be trouble looming.

"You were always different," Elizabeth was saying with a smile in her eyes. "You were like me, the daughter I should have had. Don't ask me where Cerise got her wildness. Neither her father, rest his soul, nor I were like that. But you...you have the best of us. It is truly a miracle that you managed to escape both Cerise and Alex."

"As I recall, they escaped me," Corinne quipped with one brow arched.

"I'm referring to inherited traits. You have nothing of either of your parents, thank heavens."

"I have mother's hair and her eyes. And the Fremont nose." Corinne put a finger to the tiny bump on its bridge. Over the years, that bump had come to serve as a reminder of something wayward, something Corinne didn't want. Now she rubbed it as though to make it disappear. It didn't, of course, and she frowned.

But Elizabeth was as oblivious of the frown as she was ignorant of what had put it there. "You have my mind and my temperament. Those are the important things." She paused. "Have you heard from your mother lately?"

"Not since last month, but you saw that postcard yourself. As far as I know, she's still in Dubrovnik."

"What she's doing in Yugoslavia is beyond me, but then, Cerise is beyond me in every respect."

"I'm told the beaches there are lovely."

"She didn't say who she was with."

"No."

"I suppose it's too much to hope that she's with your father."

Corinne marveled that her grandmother could maintain that same tranquil tone of voice. Corinne certainly couldn't, though Lord only knew she'd spent enough years trying. In the end she'd given up. There weren't many things that brought a bite to her words, but the matter of her parents was one. "I believe Alex is still in Paris. Mother met some duke or count there. They've been traveling along the Dalmation Coast together."

"Who's footing the bill?"

"I assume the duke or count or whatever. When they tire of each other, she'll join Alex again."

Elizabeth shook her head, and the sadness in her eyes was nearly tangible. "It's a strange relationship they have—together, apart, here, there. You'd think that they'd want to spend time with their daughters."

"They never did. Why would that change?"

"They're getting older."

Corinne had to chuckle at that. "Older? Mother is forty-seven, Alex forty-eight. I don't think they've hit the stage of looking back just yet. For that matter, I don't think they ever will."

"It's a shame. They've seen little Jeffrey once in his life, and then it was simply because they happened to be passing through New York. And you—you'd think that they'd want to know about your job. I find it impressive, myself."

"That's because you're you, Gram," Corinne said with a gentle smile, but she'd had about enough of discussing her parents. They were lost to her, and she'd long since stopped holding her breath hoping they'd be back. At this point, she didn't need them. She was grown and independent, with a life of her own making. She didn't see the point in agonizing over what she might have had once. That time for longing was past.

Rising, she carried her glass to the sink, rinsed it and placed it in the dishwasher. "Are you having lunch with Mrs. Frederick tomorrow?"

"Yes. She's invited me to her house at noon. Have you any plans?"

"I'd like to stay around, since I've been gone half the week."

Elizabeth nodded, then stood and started for the door. "You won't forget to water the plants?"

"No, Gram."

"And do the towels and sheets? If the sun's out, they'll dry in no time. I know that the dryer is quicker, but no detergent smells as sweet as the outdoors."

"I'll take care of it."

"And the magazine rack needs weeding out. I'd do it myself, but I never know what you want to keep. We've passed the three-month mark on some of those issues."

Corinne smiled at her grandmother's timetable. "Done."

"Such a good girl," Elizabeth said, and blew Corinne a kiss. "Good night, dear."

"Good night, Gram."

Corinne waited until she heard her grandmother's door close upstairs before shutting off the kitchen lights and returning to the hall for her bag. She still had her sister's letter, open but unread, in her hand. Tucking it under her arm, she lifted her bag and climbed the stairs to her own room.

The room, the house, her grandmother—all had a feeling of normalcy about them. Yet, something was different. Putting Roxanne's letter on the dresser, she methodically hung up her clothes, went into the bathroom and showered. As always, she reached for the towel on the right. As always, when she returned to the bedroom, she turned down the left side of the bed and checked, then rechecked the alarm clock.

But she was forgetting something—not really forgetting it, but putting it off. Her eye fell on her travel bag. She stared at it for several minutes, then slowly crossed the room, lifted it to the bed and opened it.

Pandora's box couldn't have been more jam-packed. All of the thoughts and emotions Corinne had pushed to the back of her mind since entering the house came forth in a rush with the sight of that one, dark blue T-shirt dress resting on top. Feeling stunned and more than a little weak, she left the bag unzipped and sank down on the bed beside it.

Three and a half days. Was that all it had been? It seemed like an aeon since she'd left Baltimore and flown to South Carolina, though she couldn't say that time had dragged while she'd been there. To the contrary, she looked back on it as a whirr of activity, productive and satisfying where work was concerned.

Where work wasn't concerned ... therein lay the aeon. In slow motion and vivid detail, she recalled everything that had happened to her since her phone had rung early that morning. Lying back on her bed, eyes on the ceiling, she then replayed it all a second time. Had she been a fly on that ceiling returning her gaze, she would have seen the way her cheeks flushed, the way her breasts rose and fell more quickly, the way her lips parted and her eyes became half-lidded.

Then she closed them and took a shuddering breath. Indeed, something was different and that something was Corinne, herself. She'd learned a truth about herself today that she'd hoped she'd never learn.

*You have nothing of your parents, thank heavens,* Elizabeth had said. But that wasn't quite true, Corinne had discovered.

Once again she remembered how Corey had held her, how he'd kissed her and touched her. She remembered how she'd wound her fingers through his hair, how she'd kissed him back, how she'd let him touch her and then begged him to do it again.

Eyes squeezed tightly shut, now, she gave a violent shake of her head, but the images wouldn't fade any more than would the raw facts.

She'd enjoyed herself. In disregard for every vow she'd ever made to herself, she'd submitted to, then welcomed Corey's passion, and she'd enjoyed it. Even now, her body tingled with remembered pleasure. She hadn't dreamed a man's touch could be that way; she hadn't *allowed* herself to dream it.

But now she knew, and she was afraid. She didn't want to like Corey, but she did. She didn't want to be attracted to him, but she was. She didn't want to think of what might have happened if he hadn't stopped in time, but she couldn't help it!

They'd have made love, and in so doing, she'd have proved herself her mother's daughter, indeed. But it wasn't the lovemaking that would have been wrong, per se. If she'd made love with Tom or Richard, it would have been fine; she would have known what she was doing, would have been in complete control of her senses.

With Corey, she wouldn't have been. He had a mystical power over her, a power no other man had ever had. She was an alien creature in his arms, while he was the Cardinal. He was a fast mover, a ladies' man, a free agent. He was danger unlimited.

And she was drawn to him, just as her mother had been drawn to her father, with a kind of mindless force that overrode rational thought. But rational thought had always been Corinne's personal catechism. She'd never jumped blindly into things. She'd always looked before she'd leaped. She'd built her life on the concept of self-control, but today she'd lost it. She'd lost sight of herself.

If only she hadn't gone to Hilton Head. But then the trouble hadn't started there. Her eyes crept stealthily, reluctantly, to her dresser. Rising from the bed, she crossed the room, opened the second drawer down and pulled from between the neatly stacked supply of new panty hose a dollar bill that had been torn into six-teenths and carefully, painstakingly taped back to-gether. She moved it between her fingers, running the pads of her fingers over the tape. Then she snapped the bill.

The tape held.

Bracing her hands on the top of the dresser, she dropped her chin to her chest and closed her eyes in bewilderment and fear.


By the following Wednesday morning, she was no closer to easing either. She hadn't heard from Corey, and while one part of her was grateful, the other was angry. She'd have thought that after what they'd shared on the boat—after the way he'd held her in his arms and told her that what they'd done was right, that she shouldn't agonize over it, that he didn't want it to end—he'd have made some attempt to contact her. The fact that he hadn't attested to the shallow-ness of his words. She was angry at that, angry that she'd fallen for him even for those briefest of mo-ments, angry that she'd thought she could trust him.

But there was still the matter of work to consider. He'd hired her to do the job that Alan had subse-quently dared her to do, and she had no intention of letting either of them think that she didn't have it in her to do that job well. After much thought she decided to take the offensive, which was why, on that Thursday morning, she lifted the phone and called Corey.

He wasn't in his office. His secretary said that he was out of town and wouldn't be back until the first of the week, but when she offered to take a message, Corinne simply said she'd call back.

Monday. It wasn't fair that she'd have to wait that long when she was psyched up to make the contact today, but then it wasn't as though she had nothing better to do with her time than sit around and think about Corey Haraden. Sublimating defiance, she applied herself to her other work with a doggedness that would have pleased Alan had he known of it. But Alan, too, was out of town, so the effort on that score was wasted.

Not so the time. She made remarkable headway on a survey she was designing for a credit card company, worked with the coders on another questionnaire that was ready for breakdown, spent hours with Jonathan Alter instructing him on the proper computer programming for yet a third study. She even returned the phone calls of two particularly impatient clients.

It was at midday Thursday, during one of those calls, that she looked up from her desk to find Corey at her door. For a minute she thought she was imagining him. So often in her mind she'd looked up to find him there that it was hard to separate fact from fiction.

"Yes, Mr. Cimino, we've done that," she said, dropping her eyes to the open folder on her desk. "The last of the questionnaires is in now, and the coders are at work."

She lifted her eyes. Corey was still there.

"Uh-huh," she went on, focusing back on the folder. "I do understand, but we're dealing with several thousand forms. We were fortunate to get as many responses—"

She blinked once and looked up. This time she held Corey's gaze.

"It will take at least a week or two to complete the coding, then another week for the analysis—" She paused, listening. "The middle of June. That's right. I'll call when we're nearing that point to set up a date for us to meet." She nodded in response to something the client said. "Fine. I'll speak with you then. Goodbye."

Slowly she replaced the receiver, neatened the papers in the folder, then closed it and sat back in her chair. She should have guessed that Corey would show up; he had a habit of doing that. But she'd worked so hard to push him out of her mind—and been successful at it that she was unprepared. It took her a minute to garner an inner poise to match that on the outside.

"Busy?" he asked.

"Always," she answered.

"May I come in?"

He was a client. She had little choice. Nodding toward the chair, she watched him cover the short space and ease down opposite her. She was grateful the desk separated them; he couldn't see how her hands were clenched in her lap.

*He looks different. Nervous.*

That's guilt.

*No. There's less of a bounce to his step. It's apprehension.*

It's guilt.

*It's caution. Can you see it in his eyes?*

All I see is sparkling green. Damn it.

"I'm sorry I haven't called," he said. "I've wanted to, but I wasn't sure how I'd be received."

*Was* it apprehension, or was that in itself an extension of guilt? "You had no cause to worry. I'm working for you. You can call whenever you want."

"I'm not thinking about work, Cori."

"I am. As a matter of fact, I tried to call you yesterday, but you weren't in the office." Swiveling her chair, she exchanged the folder on her desk with another on the credenza. Swiveling back, she opened it and began to move papers. "I've drawn up some formal plans and finished the first draft of a questionnaire. We'll have to go over them before I can move ahead."

"It was nice having you with me last week. I've missed you since then."

Corinne cleared her throat. "I'd like to go with the idea of putting questionnaires in the rooms. It occurred to me after meeting the shopkeepers and charter people that we could offer a variety of incentives in the form of discount coupons."

"I stood at the airport and watched your plane take off. I felt odd. I'm not sure I can explain it."

"We'd have to calculate in dollars and cents exactly what it would mean to those of you who are sponsoring the survey, but I have a feeling that the shopkeepers and charter people would gladly chip in, since they'd be getting business they might not ordinarily get."

Corey sat forward in his seat, his eyes as intense a green as she'd ever seen them. "Have dinner with me tonight, Cori."

She took a quick breath. "I have some time later this afternoon to discuss everything."

"I'm on my way to a series of meetings across town. I'll be late even now, but I couldn't stay away. Dinner tonight. How about it?"

"I'd... rather not."

"Why?"

"It's easier to work in the office."

"I don't want to work. I want to talk with you."

"I don't think I want that," she said very softly.

"I frighten you."

"Yes."

"I make you nervous."

"Yes."

"I make you think about things you don't want to think about."

She paused, then breathed a third yes.

Slumping back in his chair, he muttered, "At least you're honest." The eyes he trained on her were sad. "You regret what happened last Saturday, don't you?"

The sadness had extended from his gaze to his voice. She tried to tell herself that it was a deliberate ploy, but something inside her wasn't listening. She felt wrenched. Swallowing once, she nodded.

"Will you tell me why?"

"I... it just wasn't right. That's all."

"It felt right at the time."

"I wasn't thinking at the time."

"Is it so important to think? What about feeling?"

"It should go hand in hand with thinking."

"Life doesn't always work that way."

"I know. That's what frightens me."

He sat forward again and spoke with quiet urgency. "But there's nothing to be frightened of, not when you're with me. Don't you see? There's something very right about our being together." He frowned, trying to collect his thoughts, but it was hard when she was staring at him as though he was speaking Greek. Still, he tried. "You tone me down, I tone you up. It sounds like a compromise, but no compromise ever felt so comfortable to me before."

Her gaze didn't waver.

"I feel like I've been looking for you for a long time," he confessed.

"Why does that sound like a line?"

"Maybe because it's used so much, but it may just be there's some truth to it."

"Or hidden purpose."

"You think I'm trying to manipulate you."

"I think," she whispered, "that you know one part of me is susceptible."

"I do. It's that part you try to keep under lock and key."

She looked down at her hands. Her fingers were strangling each other. "I've been successful until now."

"Then, think. Why are you failing.... No, wrong word, there's nothing failing about it. Why does that susceptibility surface when you're with me?"

"I don't know."

"It's a wonderful susceptibility. It means you're warm and passionate, very human."

Her eyes flew to his. "I've always been warm and passionate and human. Sex isn't the only outlet in life."

"It's the most appropriate one when a man and woman feel the kind of attraction we do." He held up a quick hand. "Don't deny it, Cori. You've been honest this far. Don't spoil it now."

She dropped her eyes to the papers before her. "I'd really like to limit our relationship to work."

Corey, who'd done his utmost to be as reasonable and calm as she was, lost himself then. "Hell, Cori, we've gone *beyond* that. It's too late to go back!"

"Maybe someone else should handle your project."

He bolted from his seat and began to pace the floor. "I don't want that. *You* were the reason I wanted this done in the first place. No, don't give me that offended-maiden look, because we've gone beyond that, too." He stopped short at her desk and flattened his hands on the wood surface. "You want to know the truth? The truth is that, yes, I want this project done. And, yes, the information I'll get from it will be useful. But even more than that, I wanted to get to know *you.* When you wouldn't see me socially I figured I'd have to do it through work, and that was fine until last Saturday. Then pure instinct took over. I didn't plan that, Corinne. I didn't take you on the boat with the intent of seducing you. After the fact I felt that *I'd* been the one seduced."

"I never—"

"Not consciously, I know that. Just as what happened wasn't conscious doing on my part, either. I knew you were leery of me. Why do you think I kept my distance for the first two days? I wanted to give you a chance to get to know me, and that was the honest reason I took you on that boat. Things were going so well. We were talking and laughing. We were becoming friends. Do you think I would have purposely risked that for the sake of a quick kiss or a little feel—"

He wanted to take the words back the instant he said them. Then again, the stricken look in her eyes was encouraging. "Y'see," he went on more gently, "it wasn't a quick kiss or a little feel to you, either. It was something deeper and more meaningful, and the only reason, the *only* reason I regret it happening is because it's obviously upset you."

He paused and took a deep breath. "I said I was feeling vulnerable then. I've thought a lot about that feeling of vulnerability, Cori. When I met you, you intrigued me because you were different. You were quiet-spoken, poised, dignified. Then I found, little by little, that you had a sense of humor and when you smiled I felt like a million. When you opened up to me the way you did on the boat—and I'm not talking physical now—I learned something about myself. I've always thought myself free as a bird, but I wasn't. I was passing time, looking, waiting for the right woman to come along. Tell me it's a line if you want, but I think I'm falling in love with you."

Corinne's eyes widened. "You can't—"

"Maybe not, but it sure as hell feels that way. I wish it were with any other woman, because it hurts that you're so dead set against it. But I can't help the way I feel. I can't change it." He took another deep breath and straightened. "Well. I guess I've said enough." He ran a hand through his hair. "I haven't had much practice in baring my soul. Frankly, it sucks." He walked to the door, turning back only when he'd reached it. Suddenly, he looked tired and his voice held an element of defeat. "I'll be at Montague's tonight at eight. If you don't show I won't bother you again."

When he'd gone, Corinne was certain of only one thing. The work she'd feverishly done for the past day would have to stand her in good stead. It was a cinch that she'd be useless now.

# 6

Promptly at eight o'clock Corinne entered Montague's. There were several small groups of people waiting in the foyer, but Corey wasn't among any of them. Stepping unobtrusively past the others, she approached the maître d' and spoke softly.

"I was to meet Corey Haraden here. Has he come yet?"

"Miss Fremont?" At Corinne's nod, he smiled. "Right this way, please."

She followed him through the restaurant until they reached the small corner table at which Corey sat. He stood quickly, and her footsteps faltered for an instant. But where she had expected him to be smug—her presence his victory—there was only relief on his handsome, tanned face. His movements were smooth when he seated her.

"Would you like something to drink?" he asked as soon as she was settled.

"A glass of white wine would be nice."

Crooking a finger at a nearby waiter, he ordered two glasses of Chablis, then rested his arms lightly on the table. He was wearing a fresh suit and shirt, she noticed with some chagrin; she'd come straight from work and hadn't had a chance to change. Moreover, he'd shaved. *A twice-a-day man, indeed.* And his tie was neatly knotted.

"Thank you," he murmured, his eyes holding hers. "I wasn't sure you'd come."

Tearing her gaze away, she studied the ice cubes in her water glass. They hadn't had quite the cooling effect she'd hoped for. Her voice sounded strained. "I felt I owed you an explanation."

"For why you don't want anything but a business relationship?"

"For why I am the way I am." She'd thought about it all afternoon. She did believe that he'd bared a little bit of his soul to her, and she felt it only right that she do the same. Perhaps then he'd understand. Perhaps he'd make things a little easier for her. As it was, she was lost each time he looked sad, or tired, or discouraged. She knew there was another side to him, one that was totally confident, bolder and more brash, and that side she could resist with a minimum of effort. It was the other that wormed its way into her, drawing her to him when she wanted to stay away.

"I'm listening," he coaxed softly.

She knew just where to begin. She'd thought that all out, too. Eyes glued to the gleaming, scroll-handled knife by her plate, she began. "My father was an only child. By the time he was sixteen his parents had both died, but they'd left him phenomenally wealthy. From what I've been told, he was always a little wild. Then, suddenly, he was on his own with unlimited resources, so he took off. He didn't bother finishing school. He felt there was no need, because he could live handsomely on the income generated by the investment of those millions without ever having to touch the capital itself."

"Fremont. Should I know the name?"

"Only if you've ever dabbled in silver." She tapped the knife with a forefinger. "My grandfather made a mint off the stuff. He could see early on that my father wanted nothing to do with the business, so, when he took sick—that was after my grandmother died, which meant that Alex would have been free to run it into the ground—he sold it. The mint tripled overnight. He invested the money, stipulating that Alex could only use the interest."

"But it was enough."

"More than enough. Alex traveled. He partied. He wined and dined whomever, whenever. He met my mother a year after his father died. She came from a family of far lesser means and had always been rebellious herself. She was more than happy to marry Alex and be taken away from a life she felt to be stifling."

"Were they in love?"

"Could they know what love was at that age?"

"Exactly how old were they when they married?"

Corinne looked at him, then, feeling embarrassed, apologetic, resigned. "Suffice it to say that when I was born, less than a year later, she was seventeen and he was eighteen."

"Whew. A little young to be starting a family."

She lifted one shoulder, but it fell back and her head shot up when the waiter appeared with their drinks. She sipped hers for a minute, hoping it might relax her, before continuing. "They were free of all financial worry, so theoretically it could have worked. But they wanted to be free in every respect. They didn't want to be tied down by a child."

"So why did they have one?"

"Arrogance, maybe, or defiance. Maybe they felt that once they'd done their part in propagating the species, they could go on to lead the kind of lives they wanted without having to think of interruptions later."

"Who took care of you?"

"My grandmother. From the time I was one, right after my sister was born, she was our sole guardian. Oh, it was okay," she rushed on when Corey winced. "She was young, herself, only thirty-six at the time, which is when many women nowadays are having children of their own. And Alex saw to it that she had enough money to provide well for us. My mother had been so difficult for her to raise that I think Gram was glad to have been given a second chance."

"She must be a remarkable woman."

"She's very precise and organized, even dogmatic. But, yes, she's remarkable."

"And your parents? What did they do once they'd left you in her care?"

"They did what they wanted, what my father had been doing before they were married. They traveled and played and had a grand time for themselves."

While Corey knew people like that, he couldn't conceive of parents like that. His own hadn't had the means, much less the wish to be separated from their children for long. "They must have come to see you often."

"Why so?" Corinne asked. Bitterness gave her voice a brittle edge. "They'd done their thing. They'd given us life. They supported us. They saw that we were well cared for."

"There's more to parenting than that."

"You and I may know it, but they certainly didn't. If they did, they chose to ignore it. They stopped by once in a while, but they never stayed long. We were like playthings. They held us and cooed a little, then handed us back to Gram and left.''

Again Corey thought of his own upbringing. His parents had always been there, hugging and holding, making up in love for what they couldn't give their children materially. "It must have been hard on you."

She shrugged. "Gram did her best."

"Where was your grandfather through all this?"

"Dead."

"Then there were just the three of you?"

"Yes." She paused, and the whisper of a frown crossed her face.

"How did you feel about that?"

"I was angry and hurt. I never let Gram see it, because I knew that she was trying to be a good parent, and she succeeded to an extent. Her heart was in the right place. But Gram is Gram. In her own quiet way, she's demanding, insistent, hard to please. I adapted to it well enough, but Roxanne was a handful so I chipped in there, too, trying to keep her under control. There were times when I wanted to run off just like my mother had done, but I felt I owed something to Gram, and I couldn't desert Roxanne."

"Some girls might have rebelled against the responsibility."

"Some might have. I went the other way. I decided that I didn't want to be frivolous and irresponsible. I didn't want to dedicate myself to a hedonistic life."

"Like your parents."

"Yes."

"Are they still alive?"

"Oh, yes, and as sybaritic as ever." Her eyes met his. "Now we get to the really disgusting part. Are you sure you want to hear it?"

Corey smiled ever so gently. "I think you don't want to say it, but I do want to hear it."

She held his gaze, as though daring him to flinch. "My parents have an open marriage. They think nothing of going off with different partners when the mood hits. When they're together Alex foots the bill. When they're apart it's to each his own. Which means that my mother is basically a well-kept mistress for a series of revolving masters. Right now she's in Yugoslavia with the man of her latest dreams. Alex is in Paris, no doubt with an equally captivating partner."

Corey hadn't flinched once. "Alex is the Silver Fox?"

She nodded. "You remembered."

"Why do you call him Alex, when you refer to your mother as Mother?"

"Respect for my grandmother. Maybe for my mother since she, at least, carried me for nine months, which was a lot more than my father did."

The blatant sarcasm at the last prompted Corey to tease, "That can't be why you're against sex."

Corinne wasn't in a teasing mood. She was coming to the harder part of her explanation, and the little bit of wine she'd had didn't seem to be helping. "I have nothing against sex," she said. "It's the lack of consideration, the absence of liability that bothers me. They were *wrong*. They shouldn't have had children if they weren't willing to parent them."

"And you? Where does that leave you? Where does it leave us?" He'd spoken very quietly, but not so much so that she missed the gravity in his tone.

Holding the stem of her wineglass, she studied the pale liquid. "I'm not frivolous and I'm not happy-go-lucky. Everything I do is done with a level head. I'm committed to my career. It's steady and stable." Her gaze rose to search his and her voice grew pleading. "I need that stability, Corey. I need to know who I'm going to be with, when and where. I need a home. One place. I need to know that I'll be sleeping there night after night." She caught a breath. "You're different. You're more spontaneous than I could ever be, and more impulsive. You thrive on excitement. And that scares me." Her gaze fell along with her voice. "What also scares me is that when I'm with you, sometimes I forget about everything I've always wanted to be. I lose control of my senses." Eyes still downcast, she tipped her head and shrugged. "I get terrified when I think of where that might lead."

Prying her fingers from the glass, he sandwiched them between both of his hands. They felt small and fragile. "You're not like your mother, Cori."

"I was last Saturday."

"No. You were like any other woman going with her feelings. Y'know, your grandmother didn't produce your mother in a vacuum. She had to have felt something for your grandfather."

Corinne gave an awkward little half laugh. "Sex isn't something I've ever associated with Gram."

"But I'm not talking only of sex. It's just one part of a relationship, at times a very minor part, and it certainly can't keep a relationship going if there's nothing else to work with. You and I have something more. Think of the time we spent together over the course of nearly four days last week. Were we compatible?"

With a one-shouldered shrug, she answered reluctantly. "We didn't fight, if that's what you mean."

"I mean more than that. We see eye to eye on the project you're doing, and let me tell you, I don't see eye to eye with everyone. Ask my secretary. She's heard the bellowing coming from my office any number of times when I've been in conference or on the phone. I'm certainly no shrinking violet. If I hadn't liked your ideas I'd have told you so in a minute. So, we're compatible where work is concerned. And we agree on our judgments of people. During the meetings you held, you picked the strong from the weak, the secure from the insecure, the leaders from the followers. We discussed it afterward, and in each case you echoed what I'd felt myself."

"But we're *different*."

"How do you know that?" he shot back, then quickly put a rein on his belligerency. "You don't really. You're clinging to an initial impression you formed, because you're afraid of involvement."

"That's right," she cried. "I am."

He brought her hand, still wrapped in his, to his chest. "Well, you shouldn't be. You should be open and curious, and one part of you is or you'd never have let me touch you the way I did on the boat." He tightened his grip when she tried to pull away, but the force with which he held her was ever gentle. "I want your mind, just as much as your body. I want you to think about me, to analyze all those things you think are so awful and ask yourself whether they're grounded in fact. My guess is they're not. My guess is that you felt threatened the first time you saw me, because even then the lure was there, so you grabbed on to every possible excuse to convince yourself that I'm no good."

"I never said you were no good," she whispered, slanting her gaze away.

"Then, not right for you. Is that more on the money?"

She nodded.

"Look at me, Cori," he begged. "Please, look at me."

His commands she could defy. Against pleading, she was helpless. Slowly she raised her eyes to his, then waited apprehensively for him to speak. It took him a while, and during that time the emerald softness of his gaze sent a heat through her that congealed not in her loins but in her heart.

"What would you say if I asked you to marry me?"

The heat dissipated. She blinked. "I'd say you were nuts."

He lowered his head, shook it slowly, then grinned up at her. "You're amazing. Here I propose to a woman for the first time in my life, and she tells me I'm nuts."

"You didn't propose. You posed a hypothetical question."

"Did I?"

"Of course. We don't know each other. I've just gone on and on about how different we are—"

"*You* have. Not me. And different doesn't necessarily mean trouble. If we were exactly alike, life together would be boring as sin."

"I *like* boring lives. I *like* constancy and predictability."

"Is that why you were having such a wonderful time on the boat when it was heeled over and there was that little bit of danger? You came alive then. I've never seen you as free."

"It was a novelty. I couldn't take a steady diet of it."

"But you're missing the point. The point is," he stated very slowly and in a lowered voice, "that you're settling for second best by refusing to take a chance. I could give you constancy and predictability, in the sense of having that home you want and financial security. I couldn't promise that you'd sleep in the same bed every night, because I have to travel for business and I like to take vacations. Not all the time, and certainly not after we had children, but when it was at all possible I'd want you with me. And I couldn't promise that I wouldn't do little things, fun things, spontaneous things, because that's the way I am. And I think you'd like those things, too."

"The waiter is hovering. I think he wants us to order."

"I would promise to be faithful to you."

Faithfulness—from the Cardinal? She aimed a skeptical squint his way. "Have you thought all this out, Corey?"

"Of course, I have."

She wasn't convinced. "And you came here tonight knowing you were going to propose marriage?"

"Well...not exactly...I didn't know if you'd show.... And if you did, there was always the chance you'd throw water or wine or whatever in my face and tell me you never wanted to see me again."

Her lips twitched. "Your neck is red."

"I feel dumb."

"And rightly so. A man doesn't just ask a woman to marry him on the spur of the moment. He has to *think* about it."

"Nuh-uh. That's where you're wrong. If he *feels* it, like he's never felt anything before, he doesn't have to think."

"He has to be fully convinced that he's making the right decision."

"He can know that in his gut, without hashing it out in his mind. I'm telling you, Cori, I want to marry you."

She tugged at her hand. "I'd better look at the menu."

"Will you marry me?"

"I think that waiter is going to ask us to leave if we don't give him our order."

"Will you?"

"Give him my order? As soon as you free my hand so I can look at the menu."

"Cori..."

"Corey?"

His brows lowered to shadow his eyes, making them look more hunter than emerald. "Do you know what you're doing? Listen to you. Theoretically you should be all in a tizzy because I'm proposing, but you're not. And you want to know why? Because you've repressed the entire issue, that's why."

"Thank you for the analysis," she said tartly, to which he only grinned and raised her hand to his lips.

"I love it when you go sour on me. It's that much more of a challenge to sweeten you up."

Corinne shut her eyes and took a deep breath. It came out with several catches. "Okay, Corey. You want to know the truth? The truth is that I feel confused and scared, and you're not helping matters any."

"Confused and scared. That I can buy. As for my not helping matters, tell me what you want me to do and I'll do it."

"Right now," she said in a tremulous voice, "I'd like you to give me back my hand. I can't think when you're kissing it."

"I'm sorry. I like the touch of your skin on mine."

It was her turn to plead. "Corey...?"

He snapped off a crisp, "Okay," and released her hand, but not before popping a final kiss on her knuckles.

She promptly opened the menu, then braced it against her plate when it shook in her boneless grasp. "This isn't going to work," she whispered more to herself than to him.

"Sure it is," Corey responded, bending his head to hers so that his own near-whisper carried easily. He was feeling suddenly light-headed, and it had nothing to do with the single swallow of wine he'd had. Corinne liked him. By her own confession, she was drawn to him. It was a start. "I tell you what. We'll table this particular conversation for a bit and just sit back and enjoy our dinner. Sound fair?"

She nodded.

"Good." He straightened. "Uh, waiter? We'll just be another minute, okay?"

Corinne could hear the smile in his voice, just as she could envision the waiter's suddenly pleasant expression. Corey would tip lavishly. He was the type. Generous, gentle, enchanting. At times it was hard to remember what she feared.

That was the case through most of the evening. True to his word, Corey steered clear of any discussion of their relationship, focusing instead on his work. He told her about the property he was currently negotiating for in Baltimore, on which he hoped to build a hotel and shopping complex, and about similar property in Cleveland, where construction was already under way. He told her about various others of his projects, even shared the dream he had of going international at some point. He invited her opinion on everything he said, and she offered it. Though she had some reservations about the wisdom of trying for a sports arena in Boston, where the idea had been hashed around and nixed for years, by and large she could find little fault with his plans and certainly none at all with his enthusiasm.

Too soon, they finished their second cups of coffee and left the restaurant. Corey guided her to a waiting cab, settled her inside, then slid in next to her.

"Address?" he inquired softly.

"Wherever you're staying. I can drop you at your hotel, then go on to my house." There was nothing unusual about the arrangement; it was what she often did when she was working with out-of-town clients. She'd always felt it dignified to play the part of hostess that way, and she would have been pleased to do so now.

Corey would have none of it. "I'll drop you home, then go on to my hotel. What's your address?"

"It's really not necessary, Corey. Your hotel is bound to be closer. It's ridiculous for you to take me all the way home, then come back."

"I *insist*."

"But it's late. You have meetings tomorrow."

"So do you. And I don't like the idea of sending you off alone at this time of night."

"It's not like I'm on a public bus. I'll be perfectly safe—"

"Where to?" came the gruff call from the front seat of the cab.

With a punishing glance at Corinne, Corey leaned forward and proceeded to give the cabbie her address. Then he sat back and waited for her response. He had to wait a little longer than he expected, but he reminded himself this was Corinne. He wasn't looking at her, but he could feel her taking a deep breath, see her pursing her lips, imagine the way she'd be counting to ten before speaking quietly, calmly, deliberately. When she said nothing at all, he was unsettled.

"I looked it up in the phone book, okay?" He sounded embarrassed yet defiant, like a little boy caught stashing the valentine he'd written to his puppy love under the socks in his bureau. "Men do things like that when they're head over heels in love."

"This afternoon, you only *thought* you were in love."

"I must have been feeling it before then," he said in the same begrudging tone. "I looked up your address when I was here two weeks ago."

"You don't sound very happy."

"How should I sound? You don't want me to see your house."

"It's not that...."

"It's your grandmother then. You don't want her to meet me. She must be one hell of a soft-spoken dragon lady if you're so sure she'll disapprove of me. Are you afraid of her?"

Corinne didn't want to answer. She wasn't sure how to. She was thirty years old, an independent adult. She wasn't afraid of Elizabeth. On the other hand, she respected the woman's judgment. For reasons she wasn't ready to analyze, she didn't want to hear Elizabeth's opinion just yet.

"It's after ten. She'll be asleep."

"Then you're afraid of me," he concluded, throwing Corinne from one dilemma smack into another. "For all practical purposes, we'll be alone. Is that it?"

"I'm not afraid of you," she said, but her arms were wrapped around her middle and she was sitting firmly on her side of the back seat, her eyes trained on the night lights of the passing city.

Corey's voice was suddenly husky. "If you're not afraid, c'mere." Before she could protest he'd nestled her into the crook of his shoulder. "Just sit by me," he murmured. "We have a chaperon in the front and a limited drive ahead of us. Nothing can happen. You can think about exactly what you're doing—relaxing. You're in control. So am I."

Perhaps because of the meal they'd shared, and the wine, and the conversation, or perhaps simply because she was tired after a long and at times trying day she did just that. She relaxed against him. His shoulder supported her head, while the rest of her body conformed to his. She couldn't remember ever being so comfortable in anyone's arms. Her lids lowered, and she breathed in the essence of clean skin and raw man.

"Mmmm. Nice," he whispered into her hair. "There are times when being close is enough."

"I've missed it," she whispered, barely realizing she'd voiced her thoughts when Corey responded.

"Missed being held by me or by any man?"

It was too late to take the words back, and, besides, she reasoned, there was no real harm in them. "Missed being held, period."

"Didn't you ever have much of that?"

She shook her head. It gave her an excuse to burrow closer. Corey was so much larger than she. She felt sheltered, as though for those few short minutes she could relinquish all responsibility without being irresponsible. Even when she lay in bed at night and let go, it wasn't the same, because she was alone. Corey's presence made a difference. Yet, he was right; they had a chaperon and a limited amount of time. Nothing could happen.

But something did. She felt his lips against her hair, pressing soft kisses there. She liked the sensation, so gentle and sweet. When his cheek took the place of his mouth, she was sorry, but only for an instant, because then he was caressing her forehead with those same soft kisses. She luxuriated in them, savored them, then smiled. Placing a hand on his chest for leverage, she tipped back her head.

"I thought being close was enough," she teased.

His voice was thick. "It was then. It isn't now. Kiss me, Cori. Just once. Nothing more. Just a kiss."

She wanted it. His eyes warmed her through the darkness. The intermittent play of the streetlights revealed the tenderness of his expression. Mesmerized by both the warmth and the tenderness, she raised tentative fingers to his cheek.

"Okay," she whispered.

"Come up here."

He was giving her control, letting her take the lead. She liked that. It made her feel as if she knew what she was doing.

Turning into him more, she stretched up a bit until her lips touched his. It was a butterfly touch, a testing of waters she found so soothing that she immediately returned for more. His lips were parted, but he made no move to engulf her, so she dabbled leisurely and enjoyed every minute. His mouth was smooth and pliant. She sampled its shape and texture from one angle, then another. Their breath mingled, shallow little gasps that punctuated her exploration in a way that made each touch, each caress a little more exciting than the last. She wondered if he tasted as wonderful as he felt, so she ran the tip of her tongue over his lips, then, venturing farther, over the moistness within.

The trembling arms that crushed her to him put an end to her play. "Cori!" he rasped. "Do you *know* what you're doing?"

Her voice was wispy. "You taste like coffee with cream and sugar." Which was just what they'd had before they'd left the restaurant, only what had been in her cup then hadn't tasted like Corey.

His arms tightened even more, and his breath wheezed across her forehead. "You are amazing!"

A semblance of awareness broke through her daze. Her eyes opened, then grew wide. "Shouldn't I have done that? Was it wrong?"

"Oh, no," was his moaning response, "it wasn't wrong. It was right. Too right." He slid her hand to his hammering heart. "Feel that? That's what you do to me. And this—" He started to slide his hand lower, then stopped. He wanted her fingers on him so badly that he ached, but he knew she wasn't ready for it, so he simply shifted his pelvis in a bid for comfort and cleared his throat. "You set me on fire, Cori. When you let yourself go..."

He didn't finish the thought. He was going to say that she was a natural, but that would have been the *worst* thing to say, given the fear she had of taking after her parents. But she *was* a natural. The passion was packed so tightly inside her that the tiniest crack in its casing was enough to scald him.

Returning her hand to his heart, he spoke softly against her brow. "Are you sorry?"

"No," she whispered. She couldn't be sorry for what she'd felt. She'd slid through a tunnel of incredible pleasure and had emerged in one piece. As for what he'd felt, she was surprisingly proud to have been able to stir him that way.

"Will you do it again sometime?"

"Maybe."

"Soon?"

"I don't know."

"I liked it."

"So did I."

"And you're not sorry?"

She smiled against the lapel of his blazer. "I think I've answered that once. Try another question."

"Will you marry me?"

"Try another question."

"I can't see you tomorrow. I have a full morning of meetings here, and I'm supposed to be back at the island for another one at four."

"That wasn't a question."

"It was the preamble to the question. Which is, when can I see you again?"

"Okay, folks," came the same gruff call from the front seat. "We're here."

Neither Corey nor Corinne had noticed that the cab had stopped. Both heads shot up in surprise. Corey was the first to recover. "Come on," he said, opening his door. "Let's take a walk." He was pulling her out behind him.

"We can't take a walk," she protested in an urgent half whisper. "It's nearly midnight, and if you let the cab go you'll never get another, and you can't stay *here*."

"You're right about that," he said. Leaning back to the cab, he instructed the driver to keep the meter running. Then he straightened, put an arm around Corinne's shoulder and started up the walk toward the house. "If I stay here, I won't sleep. Either I'll attack you in the middle of the night or I'll spend the hours tossing and turning in frustration, and either way, I won't be able to function tomorrow." He stopped walking, looked up at the large Victorian house and studied it in silence for a minute. "This is you, Cori," he decided.

"Prim and proper?"

"Only on the surface. Inside, there are all kinds of exciting twists, nooks and crannies. A house like this is far more intriguing than something new and modern. Have you always lived here?"

"Yes."

"You must have had a ball when you were little—playing in the attic, hiding in the closets, sliding down the banister—it does have one, doesn't it?"

"Oh, yes. Long and mahogany, curved at the base. But I've never slid down it. In Elizabeth Strand's house, one doesn't slide down banisters."

"Pity. It would be fun." He shifted his gaze. "How much land is there?"

"Nearly two acres." The light of the moon illumined both the landscape and her gesturing hand. "The property line goes way back beyond those trees."

They started walking again, Corey's arm anchoring her to his side. He sucked in a breath when they rounded the side of the house and got a full view of the backyard. "A gazebo! That's *great*!"

"Mmm. Even us prim and proper Victorians have an appreciation of the finer things in life."

He caught her hand and broke into a trot. "Come on. I want a closer look."

Corinne ran alongside him and followed him up the three steps. She was laughing by the time they reached the center of the gazebo. Though she'd come to take the place very much for granted, his enthusiasm was contagious. His eyes made a sweep of the rafters before falling to the trellised walls. "I love it," he declared with a satisfied nod. "This is where we're going to be married."

"Corey..."

"I know. You haven't said yes." He slid his arms around her, looping them loosely at the small of her back. "But you will. Sooner or later, you will."

She might have been humoring him, but she was feeling heady, herself. She tipped up her face to his. "What makes you so sure?"

"Because I love you, and you love me."

"I don't love you."

"You like me, don't you?" When she didn't deny it, he went on. "Like is the beginning of love."

"It is not. What an idiotic thing to say."

"Uh-uh. I can feel it."

"Oh? Where? In your gut again?"

"There . . . and other places." He drew her close for a demonstration, but the demonstration was like none she'd ever known. Eyes locked with hers, he inched her back and forth against him. At first she was only aware of the large hands at her hips and the solid musculature of his thighs. Then, little by little, she felt the force of his sex.

"That's lust," she croaked, but she didn't pull away.

"Made all the more potent by love." His deep voice washed over her, gravelly and intense. "When I look at you, something inside me goes all soft and shaky, even when my body's rock-hard, like it is now."

She sucked in a breath. "The cab's waiting."

"I do love you, Corinne. You're like no other woman I've ever known. I could spend a lifetime trying to explore all the little complexities in you, and even then I'd probably miss a few."

"Don't say things like that."

"I like saying them. I like standing here with you, having you cradle me the way you're doing."

Her hands were on his shoulders, fingers bunching the fabric of his blazer. "Corey . . ."

"I like kissing you, too. Like this—" he ducked his head and smacked her cheek "—and this." He popped a kiss on one eye. "And this—" he blubbered a wet one on her ear, then took the entire lobe into his mouth.

Then he made a gurgling sound, which turned into a choking sound. His hands fell away and he keeled over onto the wood planks by her feet.

"Corey! My God!" She was on her knees, snaking a trembling hand under his head. "What is it?" His eyes were closed, and his throat was working furiously. "What am I supposed to *do*? Oh my God...Corey!"

Just as she was about to pry open his lips and rescue his tongue from being swallowed, the bobbing at his throat ceased.

He opened an eye, then grinned. One large, round, pale blue button earring was clamped gallantly between his teeth.

For an instant Corinne stared at him in shock. She couldn't believe it! He'd been *playing*! She simply couldn't believe it!

With a feral growl, she snatched the earring, tossed it blindly away, then grabbed handfuls of his hair and shook him. "How could you *do* that, Corey Haraden?" she shrieked. "I thought you were *dying* and you could have, rolling the earring around like that. And lying on your back, too! That was a stupid, selfish, childish thing to do!"

"Werc you scared?"

"I was terrificd!"

"That's 'cause you love me and can't bear the thought of anything happening to me." Not only was he remorseless, he was positively smug.

"Right now," she stated between clenched teeth, "I could very happily tear apart one of those trellises and beat you over the head with it."

"Violence is once-removed from passion," he growled, "and I lo-ve a passionate woman." With that he flipped over, trapping Corinne beneath him. "Now I have you where I want you."

"Let me up, Corey." She was pushing at his shoulders. It was a futile gesture.

"Not until you kiss me."

"I kissed you before. Let me up."

He pinned her wrists to the planking by her shoulders. "Kiss me again, and maybe I'll consider it."

"The cab's waiting."

"He's being paid to wait."

"It'll cost a fortune."

"I have a fortune."

"Corey...let...me...up." The words were spoken slowly and there was a breathlessness to them that had nothing to do with the weight of Corey's body. And everything to do with it. He was firm and lean, every line and sinew imprinting itself on her with devastating effect. She'd never felt a man as intimately. She'd never been tempted to do so. And if temptation was the root of all evil, then she was evil, because, heaven help her, she didn't want to move.

His mouth was a breath from hers. "Kiss me."

"You're a brute."

"I know." But that was all he said, because the distance was gone and his lips covered hers, treating her to the same kind of kiss she'd given him in the cab, and then some. He caressed, he sucked, he nibbled. His mouth had a way of making her own melt away, so that she had to offer more and more of herself in compensation.

Her hands were no longer pinned to the floor but in his hair again, not to shake him now, but to hold him closer. And with his own hands free, he had taken his weight on one elbow while he touched her jaw, her chin, her throat.

"You are so beautiful to me," he whispered against her lips. When he kissed her again, his hand lowered to touch her breast.

She jerked, stunned by the instantaneously electrical sensation.

"It's okay," came his muffled whisper. "I'll just touch. You know what I'm doing. I'll just touch, and I want you to think of how good it feels."

It felt so good that Corinne couldn't muster the will to make him stop. When his hand circled her breast she whimpered into his mouth. When he covered it with his hand and began to gently knead it, she felt herself swell. When he raked his fingertips ever so lightly over her nipple, she arched up. It was the same electricity as before, yet different, because it surged straight to her womb.

Frightened by the strength of that surge, she cried out his name.

"Shhhh," he whispered. "It's good. It's my way of saying I love you to every hidden spot in your body."

The words, ah, the words. And their tone, and the vibrancy of his hair in her fingers, and the rising lure of his body. She whispered his name again when she felt his hands on the buttons of her blouse, but it was in a plea to hurry, not to stop.

The air of the warm May night touched her skin, followed quickly by Corey's fingers. He continued to kiss her, but they were both breathing heavily. His tongue surged deeply, tangled with hers, withdrew on a gasp.

"Like silk you are...smooth and fine...ahhh, Cori, it's so good to touch you this way...." Cupping her head with one hand, he looked down at her. "Do you feel it?" His hand covered the cup of her bra, fingers steadily, stealthily encroaching on the upper lace. "Do you know how precious you are?"

"I like it when you touch me," she whispered. "Kiss me again, Corey...."

He took her mouth in a mind-drugging kiss at the same time that he released the front catch of her bra. His hands trembled as they eased it away, and then the warmth of his fingers found her naked breasts, and his own body was the one to jerk.

She gulped for air.

"I know," he breathed. His hips were moving slowly against hers, finding the niche that her weakened thighs had instinctively spread and offered. "I love you, sweetheart. . . . Oh, Lord . . ." With the convulsive lowering of his head, he opened his mouth on her breast. His tongue laved the swollen flesh, then homed in to lick the turgid crest. Within seconds he'd drawn it into his mouth and begun to suckle.

Corinne had never imagined such pleasure, such heat, such frustration. His breath sent tingles over her breast, but the action of his mouth and tongue sent the ripples far deeper. There was so much more that she wanted; she ached for the kind of completion that only Corey could offer.

He moaned softly, then raised his head until it was on a level with hers. "I do love you," he whispered hoarsely, "so much that I can't get enough . . . and it isn't lust . . . it's this incredible need to be part of you." His hands framed her face, while his hips thrust gently, rhythmically against her. "Do you want me, Cori?"

"I want . . . something. . . ."

Her skirt was bunched up around her thighs. One of his hands fell to its hem and slid upward along her heated flesh. He lifted his hips enough to allow access, then began to stroke her through the silk of her panties.

She clutched his arms and her head fell to the side, eyes squeezed shut against the sweetest of pain. Mindlessly she arched against his hand. "Corey... I want..."

"I know." He was watching her, loving the way her lips parted, the way her breath came in tiny spurts, the way her features were tight in pleading. He dropped his gaze to her breasts, pearly in the moonlight, and he thought he'd never seen anything as beautiful. "All woman," he whispered in awe, "my woman."

Corinne wouldn't have dreamed of arguing. She was concentrating on feeling, leaving the thinking to him. She trusted him to do that, because they were working as a team, and the only thing she was thinking was that what she was feeling felt right.

Suddenly, though, something was wrong. His hand had left her. She made a soft moan in protest, but the tiny sound didn't bring him back.

"We have to stop," he said in a pained voice. "Sweetheart, we have to stop."

"Why? I don't want—"

"Right now you don't, but that's because you're not thinking." He levered himself to the side and savored a final view of her body. She was petite all over, yet the aura of passion that encompassed her disheveled state was far from diminutive. Eyes on her breasts as they rose and fell in torment, he rationalized. "You'll be thinking later, certainly tomorrow, and you'll have regrets." He reached out to touch her, then thought better of it. Coming to his knees, he set to work refastening her bra. His fingers shook. "We'll make love, sweetheart, but when we do, I want it to have been a conscious decision on your part. I don't want any regrets where our love is concerned.'' Button by button he closed her blouse.

Corinne lay in a state of confusion. Her body resented those buttons, yet her mind praised the hands that fastened them. Bit by bit she was emerging from a sensual fog and beginning to function rationally again, which was not to say that if Corey suddenly reversed his painstaking dressing of her, she'd protest. But she knew he'd made up his mind. She could see it in the taut lines of his face, lines attesting to many of the same feelings of ambivalence she was suddenly experiencing herself.

When he held out a hand, she took it and let herself be drawn to her feet. He draped an arm around her shoulders; her own settled comfortably around his waist. Side by side they headed toward the cab.

''This is the second time you've brought me to my senses,'' she said. Her confusion had gone beyond the war between body and mind, and was now wholly one of the intellect. She'd never have expected Corey to be the one to exert self-control, yet he'd done it once on the boat and again now. It didn't fit the image she'd formed of him. Strange, how he'd praised her for her judgment of people. At the moment she wondered if she was so deserving. She was feeling a good many doubts on that score; she wasn't sure she trusted herself to guess at his innermost motives. She needed to confront him, to hear his explanation. ''Why, Corey? Is there something about me that makes you hesitant?''

His pace didn't falter when he bent his head and set a gentle kiss on her brow. ''You haven't been listening to what I've said, or you wouldn't be asking that.''

"If I wasn't thinking I could hardly be listening. Tell me again."

"There's nothing wrong with you, if that's what you fear. It's just the opposite. Everything is so nearly right that I don't want to take any risks. When things are perfect, you'll know. And when that happens, you'll want to make love, really want it. Not in the heat of passion, but before we've ever touched one another."

"But why did you stop? I mean, *you*. I thought I was the one with a monopoly on self-control, but I'm not. You're the one who's had it all when we've been together."

"And that's what puzzles you? That I have self-control when you don't?" He gave a coarse laugh. "Believe me, babe, it's not for lack of wanting. I thought I'd proved that to you."

"And still you stopped."

"One of us had to. Maybe I'm trying to prove something else to you." His tone grew solemn. "Maybe I'm trying to show you that I'm not the rutting beast you supposed me to be. I'm not a beast, Cori. I may have acted the part sometimes in the past, but I've never been in love before. You're right. With another woman I doubt I'd have stopped, not when I burned the way I did just now. But you're not another woman. You're you. And when I'm with you, things are different. I'd like to think that I've finally grown up. One thing's for sure, I'm not at all uncomfortable with the new me."

They'd reached the front door of the house. Though the upper floor was dark, a soft light beamed from the inner hall. "Have you a key?" he asked softly.

Still trying to assimilate what he'd said, she fumbled in her purse. The key had no sooner appeared when he took it from her, opened the door and pressed the key back in her hand. "I'll give you a call between meetings tomorrow. Okay?"

Eyes puzzled, she nodded.

Then he smiled. It was a gentle smile, but it seemed to light up the entire porch. "'Night, Cori."

"Good night," she whispered, but she was standing still, mesmerized by that light that was inside her now.

He arched both brows. "Cori?" He made a scooting motion with his fingers toward the inside of the house.

"Oh." Stepping inside, she turned to receive the tail end of his smile before he loped off toward the cab. Softly she closed the door and leaned against it, then, in a burst of movement, whirled and whipped it open again.

But the taillights of the cab were all she saw before they, too, were gone.

She hadn't thanked him for dinner.

Even worse, she hadn't given a thought to work.

# 7

Corinne lay in bed that night taking stock of her life.

She was thirty years old. She had a fine job, a fine home and fine friends. She had a grandmother who loved her, a sister who needed her and a pair of parents who were indifferent to her.

In a year she'd be thirty-one. She'd have a fine job, fine home, fine friends. She'd have a grandmother who loved her, a sister who needed her and parents who were indifferent.

And ten years down the road? She'd be forty, with the same job, same home, same friends. She might or might not have the grandmother, and the sister may well have gotten over her need. The parents, well, the parents weren't worth considering.

Something was missing, something personal, warm and fruitful, like a husband and family. She wanted them; she'd known it for years but had pushed the thought aside. First she'd been busy with school, then starting out in a career. When she'd dated, she'd dated men with whom she'd felt safe. Not one of them had made her think of a husband and family.

Until Corey.

Corey wasn't safe. He was as different from the other men she'd known as night was from day. He made her laugh and go weak-kneed. He brought out the side of her she'd never wanted to see.

Still, he made her think of a husband and family.

In his own, inimitably frank way he'd suggested that she was settling for second best because she was unwilling to take a risk, and maybe he was right. She'd taken risks in her life, but they'd always been calculated ones. She'd thought them out beforehand, weighed the pros against the cons and reached a rational decision. That was the way she lived, the way she worked—weeding out the facts, analyzing them, drawing conclusions, then acting.

Corey Haraden's case was a tough one because she was stuck at the very first stage. She couldn't begin to weed out the facts.

*What's to weed out? He's charming, successful and dedicated.*

Right. He charms waiters, waitresses and cabbies. He's successful at wheeling and dealing in the office. And he's dedicated to getting me into bed.

*That's because he loves you.*

So he says. But is it a ploy?

*Would he spend as much time and effort on you if it was just a ploy?*

I'm a challenge, that's all. Once he's conquered me, he'll turn tail and run.

*How do you know that?*

He's admitted that he's had women right and left.

*Would you rather he be a virgin? Then you'd think there was something wrong with him.*

He could have done things in . . . in moderation.

*Corey doesn't do that. He's an all or nothing man. If you ask me, that's what real dedication is about.*

I'm not asking you.

*Then ask yourself. Would you rather he do things halfheartedly? Is that the way you want him to love you?*

I *don't* want him to love me.

*No?*

No.

It was a lie, and Corinne saw through it almost immediately. Lying there in her prim white nightgown on her starched white sheets, staring at the stark white ceiling, she realized that she did want him to love her. She wanted his love to be so strong that it could overcome every other temptation in life. She wanted it to be so strong that he couldn't bear to be apart from her. And she wanted it to be so strong that it would fully satisfy every craving, every wish, every desire she might have for the next hundred years.

He believed that he loved her now, but she wasn't convinced it would last. Worse, if she let herself love him back, would *that* last? Thanks to Corey, she'd learned that she was her parent's daughter, indeed. She loved being in his arms. He made her feel precious, feminine and alive. She wanted desperately to make love with him. But would it stop there? Once she tasted the forbidden fruit, would she need more and of greater variety—the way her parents did?

She thought again about her life now, then thought about what life could be with Corey. The difference was truly one of hues. Her life now was black, white, sedate and neutral, while life with Corey could have the excitement of every color in the rainbow.

It could also be garish.

Was it worth the risk?

Corey sat through his meetings the next morning with only half of his mind on work. The other half was on Corinne. He was remembering his initial impression of her that day at Alan's and how it had changed. What he'd thought of as skinny was gaminelike, what he'd thought of as boyish was delicately feminine. She was slender at places, full at others—so much like a young bud waiting to bloom that he grew taut at the prospect. He saw now that even her short, neat hair worked in her favor, for it bared the fine lines of her face, the character of her nose, the myriad emotions in her deep-brown eyes.

When he'd first seen her, he'd thought her average. Now he understood that what might have been average with another woman was subtlety with Corinne, and while subtlety had never been his own strong suit, he was fast coming to appreciate it. No small part of the appreciation related to the fact that he was aware of that subtlety as other men weren't. He knew of the capability of those eyes to express pleasure, fear and confusion, just as he knew of the passion that lay in wait within that small, lithe body. She was a woman of contradictions, epitomized by the lacy underwear she wore beneath her very proper clothes. Conservative on the outside, wild on the inside. Controlled without, passionate within.

But the passion wasn't only physical. Yes, she'd be an unsurpassed lover, but he knew without doubt that she'd dedicate herself to him, to their home and their children with the same undiluted passion.

Ironically, the passion that promised heaven was the great stumbling block they faced. Corinne had spent the better part of her life trying to deny the vibrant life inside her. While he'd managed to shoot a few holes in that wall of denial, he knew that if they were to have any chance of happiness together, she'd have to learn to accept herself and trust that what she felt was healthy and good.

To that end, he realized, she needed time. Time with him, learning to know him and love him. Time with herself, learning that self-denial was both unnecessary and counterproductive.

The matter of which should come first—time with him or with herself—was the simplest of the decisions he had to make that day. Shortly before noon, following a meeting he'd barely managed to fidget through, he called her.

"Hi, Cori."

She was silent for a minute. Then, slowly, she said, "You must be taking a coffee break."

He could hear the hint of dry humor in her voice that he'd come to know, yet it was different. There was a warmth to it that hadn't been there before, an intimacy suggesting a secret shared between them. And there was a faint breathlessness that wouldn't have been noticeable had he not been attuned to every nuance of her tone.

Without realizing he'd been holding his own breath, he let it out softly. "Any more coffee and I'll be ricocheting off the walls. Actually, I'm between meetings. Can't say I've been terribly effective."

Corey? Not effective? "I don't believe that." One look from those green eyes of his and he had the world on a string. She knew she wasn't the only one susceptible.

"Believe it. And speaking of work, I blew it with you, too."

She nodded, then realized that he couldn't see her. "I know."

"The worst of it is that I can't do anything about it now. I'm on my way to a lunch meeting, then to the airport. Why don't you fly down for the weekend?"

"Uh . . ."

"Okay. Next week, then. You and I can go over the stuff, you can make any revisions you want—my secretary will be at your disposal—and then we can meet with the others for final approval."

"That sounds good," she said softly. The thought of returning to Hilton Head brought a little unsureness, but it also brought excitement and the knowledge that, even apart from work, she had to see him again if she was to make headway on her personal dilemma.

"Monday? Tuesday?"

"How about Wednesday?"

He groaned. "That's five days off."

"I need it," she whispered, praying he'd understand.

He did, but it made him nervous. He'd wanted time with her to take their relationship further before she had that time to herself to wallow in her doubts. But he couldn't force her.

"Okay. Wednesday. As early in the day as possible?"

She conceded, and not only for his sake. "I'll try."

Corey didn't bother to suggest that she call in with her flight plans. He knew he'd be talking with her regularly; it wasn't so much part of any conscious plan as his simple need to hear her voice.

What surprised him during the following four days was that nothing he did was part of any conscious plan. When he sent long-stemmed white roses to her house on Saturday, it was with the spontaneous thought that one pure American beauty deserved a dozen others. When he had a basket of freshly baked croissants delivered to her on Sunday, it was because he got a sudden urge to envision her tearing apart the buttery layers with her teeth—with a passion to offset purity.

The conscious part of it came after the fact, when he realized that her grandmother would see and enjoy the roses, perhaps have one of the croissants. He was sure that Corinne wouldn't have mentioned him yet to her. If he was forcing that issue—no way could Elizabeth Strand, as Cori had described her, not question who'd sent the goodies—he felt he was doing so in a way that couldn't possibly be offensive.

On Monday morning, he sent a Baccarat bud vase to Corinne's office, on Monday afternoon, a single baby rose to go in it. This one was yellow because he thought of her as sunshine. The vase was simple, with clean-cut lines that spoke of refinement and good taste because she had both of those traits, and he loved her for them.

On Tuesday he sent nothing but his love, conveyed in an early morning phone call to her house.

"Am I calling too early?" he whispered.

She laughed softly. "No chance of that. Gram is out in the garden, and I'm getting ready to leave for work."

"Then I'm glad I caught you." His voice was back to normal, which was to say that it had a gentle jauntiness to it. "I just wanted to tell you something before you get going at the office."

"Something's come up between last night—" which was when he'd called last "—and this morning?"

"No. I just wanted to say it."

She waited. His presence flowed across the miles, soothing her in ways she wouldn't have imagined. "Yes?" she finally asked, when she needed to hear his voice again.

"I miss you."

"Corey. You called to tell me that?"

"Uh-huh. I didn't say it last night. And I wanted you to know that I won't send anything to you today."

"Thank goodness. You've already sent enough."

"I could argue with you there, but the fact is that I don't want you to think I'm trying to buy your heart with sweet little romantic nothings."

She laughed again; she couldn't help it. Only Corey would come out and say something as endearingly blunt. "I wish I could say that I can't be bought, but I have to admit that I've been touched."

"In that case—" he began, only to be interrupted.

"Corey, no. No more flowers or vases or croissants. No more anything, or I *will* think you have ulterior motives."

"See? You've made my point, and so elegantly."

"I'm at my best in the morning," she said without thinking. She could have kicked herself when she heard his drawled rejoinder.

"So am I. Fresh, warm and ready." He didn't wait for her to scold him, instead sounding suddenly resigned. "Once I get out of bed, it's shot. But that isn't what I wanted to tell you." Resignation gave way to something so heartfelt that she wondered if the phone lines distorted it. "I just wanted to say that I'll be waiting at the airport tomorrow and that I love you."

Corinne had no sooner closed her eyes around the words when the phone went dead. She didn't bother to blame the severance on AT&T. Corey had done it, she knew. He'd wanted to spare her having to reply, perhaps spare himself having to hear her hem and haw. He'd called her once a day since she'd seen him last, and this was the first time he'd said the words. She wasn't sure if she'd missed hearing them, but when she pressed the lifeless receiver to her heart, it was racing.

If anything, the speed of her pulse was even greater when she stepped off the plane the next day and saw Corey waiting on the tarmac. She couldn't deny that she was excited to see him or that the sight of his tall, lean frame, covered by a stylish shirt and slacks, stirred her. Nor could she deny an odd pleasure that he was waiting for her and for no one else.

Still, she was nervous. The last time they'd been face-to-face had been in the aftermath of their little scene in the gazebo. Would he be thinking about that, too? Would he expect her to throw herself into his arms? She'd never been in a situation like this before, and she wasn't sure how to act. She certainly couldn't extend her hand for a businesslike handshake.

In the end, she decided to wing it. She'd never done that before either, but she had no better solution....

Taking a deep breath for courage, she went forward.

Corey met her halfway. He cupped her shoulders and smiled. "I've been waiting since dawn for the damned plane to land."

She couldn't help but smile back. "It was five minutes early."

"Which by my schedule was still six hours late. It's good to see you, Cori."

"Same here, Corey."

With a squeeze to her shoulders, he took her bag, then her hand. "The car's out front. It'll be cooler there."

Nodding, she fell into step beside him. So much for awkwardness, she mused. With his warm but low-key greeting, Corey had played her perfectly. And now, other than holding her hand, he wasn't forcing any kind of closeness. She felt surprisingly comfortable.

They didn't quite make it to the car. Just before they left the shelter of the terminal, he ushered her into a corner and abruptly set down her bag.

She was between him and the wall. Nonplussed, she frowned up at him. "I owe you something," he said. "I won't feel comfortable until I pay up."

She was as confused as ever, and her expression showed it.

Propping the lower half of his body against hers, he reached into his pocket and drew out a small, foil-wrapped candy. "One Hershey's Kiss," he announced unnecessarily, since its shape was a dead giveaway. He held it up between his thumb and forefinger, much as a magician would an egg that was about to vanish. Then he carefully peeled back the foil, removed the candy and popped it into his mouth.

Corinne's own mouth dropped open. "That's mine," she protested.

He was rolling the candy around in his mouth and looked like he was in ecstasy. "Uh-uh," he finally said. "I promised you an oversize one. This is yours."

She wasn't as quick as she should have been, because she didn't catch on until his mouth had closed over hers, and then an explosion of sensation shot through her limbs and it was too late for quickness.

Warm, creamy chocolate. Gently caressive lips. A tongue rich and sweet.

She was the one who'd melted by the time he raised his head.

"There," he murmured. "How was that?"

She took a long, shaky breath. "Imaginative."

He laughed, and this time when he picked up her bag, he pinned her close to his side. "I'd planned to give you that in the car, but the plan went to hell the minute I saw you get off the plane. You should be grateful I didn't make a scene right there on the tarmac with a planeload of onlookers."

"Oh, I am," she managed, though a little voice inside her wished that he had. She was proud to be with him. She didn't know if it was the wisest thing to feel, but she couldn't help it.

"I haven't overstepped my bounds then?" he teased.

"Since when have you worried about that? As I recall, there was a little scene in the corridor of my office that pretty much mortified me."

"That was because I didn't know you at the time. If I'd realized I'd made you so uncomfortable—"

"You *wanted* to make me uncomfortable."

"Well...maybe just a little.... But I was frustrated because you wouldn't give me the time of day."

"Is that what I'm giving you now?" They'd stopped at the car, and she was searching his face looking for smugness, arrogance, anything that might give her a clue as to his feelings. He'd said that he loved her. She needed reassurance that it wasn't all a game with him.

"Right now," he said softly, "you're giving me a great deal of pleasure simply by being here. How 'bout we leave it at that."

She was more than amenable to the idea, particularly when it was such an undemanding one. Moreover, it seemed to be heartfelt, and Corey's actions over the next few days reinforced it. He smiled at her often, warming her with his deep, emerald gaze, and whenever he could, he touched her—held her hand, squeezed her elbow, draped an arm over her shoulders. There was no repeat of the heated scene in the gazebo. Other than those innocent touches, he seemed determined to show her that her presence was enough.

In other ways he was more insistent. When he took her to her hotel room to change, she found that he'd given her the same lavish suite she'd had before. She tried to protest.

"A simple room would have been fine, Corey. This is too much."

"What's too much? Instead of a room, you have a suite."

"With three vases of fresh flowers, a landscaped sun deck and a Jacuzzi?"

"Can I help it if my suites are fancy?"

"But you're wasting money on me."

"It's mine to waste as I choose."

"But—"

"Cardinal Rule Number Two. Never argue with the boss."

"That was Cardinal Rule Number One."

"And every bit as final."

She took the suite and enjoyed every minute of the time she was there, though that wasn't very much. Corey took her to dinner that night, then to a folk concert on the pier in Harbortown.

On Thursday morning they closeted themselves in his office and went over Corinne's plans for the survey from top to bottom. Corey questioned one or two points, but in each case he did so pensively, and in each case he had ready suggestions for alternatives.

After they'd gone over the questionnaire in detail, she was ready to fine-tune the changes. He insisted she use his office.

"But you need it," she protested.

"We can share it."

"There's only one desk. I'll be in the way."

"It's a big desk, and we've been sharing it all morning. Besides, you're a little bit of a thing. You could never be in the way."

"Really, Corey, a small room, or one of the secretaries' desks would be fine."

"You're staying here."

"But—"

"Cardinal Rule Number Three. Never argue with the boss."

"That was Cardinal Rule Number One...and Number Two."

"Now it's Number Three." He pressed her into his high-backed leather chair, stuck a pencil in her hand and pointed to the papers on the blotter. "Work," he commanded.

She completed the revisions. Cardinal Rule Number Four was invoked when she argued that she could type them up herself. His secretary did the typing and had copies made.

On Friday morning she and Corey met with the other islanders who had joined him in contracting the survey, and on Friday night he sat with her in a private corner of the hotel's elegant dining room to celebrate the project's enthusiastic reception. When she swore that she couldn't have another sip of champagne, he called on Cardinal Rule Number Five. When she tried to refuse the chef's walnut cheese cake, Cardinal Rule Number Six was enforced.

Corinne was just light-headed enough—and badly enough in need of fresh air and exercise—to agree without argument when Corey suggested they take a walk on the beach. Images of a surf-side tryst lurked in a hazy corner of her mind. Corey discarded his shoes and socks and rolled up his trousers to the knee, just as she'd imagined he'd do. She took her own shoes off and hung them by their sling-backs from her pinkie, just as she'd imagined she'd do. No, that was wrong. She hadn't imagined herself doing this, but some other, more daring woman. And they started to walk.

There was no surf-side tryst, just an hour of strolling hand in hand along the ocean's edge. They said little, for little was needed when the moon was playing cat and mouse with the clouds, occasional heat lightning lit the horizon and the tide lapped tiny waves of froth on their toes.

It was all so serene and romantic in such a subtle way that words would have done as much of an injustice as kisses would have done.

Corinne slept more peacefully that night than she had in days. When morning came and Corey put her on the plane heading back to Baltimore, the only thing to disturb that peace was a vague sense of unfulfillment somewhere deep inside.

Two weeks passed before she returned to Hilton Head. During that time Corey called her every day— often enough when she was at home to arouse her grandmother's curiosity. Flowers and croissants were one thing, easily attributable to Corey's appreciation for her work. Near-nightly phone calls were something else entirely.

Corinne was in the parlor after one such call. It was nine-thirty. She'd been relaxing with her thoughts when her grandmother settled into the Queen Anne chair nearby and straightened the folds of her velvet robe.

"That was Corey Haraden, I take it," she said in her pleasant, undemonstrative way.

"Uh-huh."

"He's been calling quite a bit. Tell me about him."

Corinne wasn't quite sure what to say. Mentally she'd run through a variety of scenarios of this very discussion. Somehow, none of them had seemed right. "What would you like to know?" she asked quietly.

"You've already told me where he lives, what he does and that he is a client. It's not every client, though, who sends flowers and pastries, and who calls you at home."

"No, Corey is not every client."

"What is he?"

"He is . . . a very nice man."

"Like the other men you've dated?" The question was posed evenly, though the look in Elizabeth's eyes was far from bland. It bore a faint chiding, but was offset by an element of humor that brought a chagrined smile to Corinne's lips.

"No, Gram. Corey isn't like the other men I've dated."

"I'm pleased to hear that."

Corinne's eyes widened. "You are?"

"They have been a bit boring, wouldn't you say?"

"I . . . thought they were pleasant enough."

"Pleasant enough doesn't make for a very satisfactory marriage."

For a split second Corinne wondered whether Corey had somehow gotten to Elizabeth. Perhaps he'd called and spoken with her while Corinne was at work or stopped by in person and charmed her, told her of his honorable intentions, won her over. If that was the case, there were advantages and disadvantages. If it wasn't the case—and Corinne believed it wasn't—her grandmother's raising the issue was that much more surprising.

"We've never discussed marriage," she replied awkwardly.

"You and Corey, or you and I?" Elizabeth asked pleasantly. "I know that you and I haven't, and perhaps it is long overdue."

Corinne felt a little foolish. After all, she was thirty. Theoretically, such a discussion with her grandmother should be unnecessary. Still, she was curious. "What do you mean?"

"I mean that there is no reason why you have to live out your life as an old maid just because your parents have turned you off to something that can be very lovely."

For the second time in as many minutes, Corinne was taken by surprise. She'd underestimated Elizabeth's perceptivity.

"You needn't look so startled, Corinne. It doesn't take a psychologist to see what you've been doing. I raised you. You and I are so very much alike that it's relatively easy for me to know what you're thinking, even when you don't speak those thoughts aloud. I see the look of disapproval on your face each time your parents come here. I hear the bitterness in your voice when you mention them. And now I see the flush on your cheeks when Corey calls and the smile you wear when he sends you things. No need to be embarrassed, dear. It pleases me to see you this way."

"It does?"

"Shouldn't it? After all, I want you to be happy."

"But I have been happy."

"In your own very narrow sphere, you have been. And now that sphere is broadening. Do you love him?"

"Gram!"

"It's a fair question."

"I know, but..."

"Do you love him?" she repeated ever so calmly.

Corinne looked at her hands, and her brow furrowed for an instant. "I think so."

"You sound reluctant."

"I didn't plan on this happening."

"You can't plan out every little detail of your life, Corinne, much as you might want to. Some of the best things happen without that planning."

"But he's so different."

"That may be precisely why you love him. Or rather why you never really felt anything for those other nice men you've dated."

"You don't understand. Corey is ... spirited."

"What else?"

"He's impulsive. He has a temper."

Elizabeth was undaunted. "Go on."

"He's always on the go, traveling from one place to another."

"Is he successful at what he does?"

"Yes."

"Then perhaps the traveling is justified." Her eyes took on the look of one who was older and wiser, yet she managed to pull it off without condescension. "Corinne, you cannot assume that being on the go is wrong just because your parents are always on the go. Alex and Cerise are two of a kind. I can't say that they're unique, because they do manage to find others with the same restlessness, the same obsession with play. But they are definitely in the minority. Your grandfather was always traveling."

"But that was for work."

"And your Corey's traveling isn't?"

"I... it is mostly, I guess."

Elizabeth's eyes grew distant. "Your grandfather was quite a man. Our love was something special. I knew that he had to be on the road, and I'd have given most anything to have him home here with me more often, but he was doing what he was best at, and he was doing it for my sake as well as his own. He may not have earned a lot of money, but we always had plenty of food on the table and we were able to splurge on little luxuries from time to time." She focused back on Corinne. "Talking to your mother, you'd never know it. She couldn't appreciate those little gifts. She always wanted more. She was very young. I'm afraid that, to this day, she hasn't grown up."

"What you felt for grandfather... Tell me more about it."

"As I said, it was special. We were young, too, when we fell in love, but times were different then. There were hard times during the war and hard times in its aftermath. We grew together. We enjoyed each little gain together. When we bought this house we thought it was a palace. And we were proud of ourselves. I couldn't have had the house without Theodore, and he couldn't have had the house without me." Her cheeks grew pink, the only sign that what she was saying was personal and had rarely been aired. "That was what he always said. He said that I was his backbone, that he wouldn't have been able to work the way he did if he didn't know that he was coming home to me."

"What a beautiful sentiment."

"It was one of many he expressed. He had a way with words, your grandfather did. Even if I hadn't already loved him to distraction, I doubt I'd have been able to hold out against his poetry. But it wasn't only the words. It was the feeling behind them. There was nothing phony about Theodore. He loved me every bit as much as I loved him."

Corinne would have liked nothing more than to have asked about their sexual relationship, but it was none of her business. Corey was right: Cerise hadn't been produced in a vacuum. Whether she'd been produced in the heat of passion was something Corinne would never know. She could hedge, though.

"You were...different with him than you were with others?"

"Oh, yes," was all Elizabeth said. Strangely, it was enough. For the first time in Corinne's memory, her grandmother's voice had grown wispy.

"I'm different when I'm with Corey."

"As well you should be. A man should have access to a side of his woman that no one else does."

"How do you explain my parents, then?"

Elizabeth's tone grew benign once again. "I don't. I can't. It is impossible for me to identify with the way they live. If I speculate, the most plausible explanation I reach is that they've never quite satisfied each other, which may be why they're driven to strangers."

"But if they love one another—"

"A big 'if,' Corinne."

"You don't think they do?"

"Maybe each in his own selfish way. Cerise's first love is herself. I would venture to say that the same is true for Alex. They certainly don't love each other the way I loved Theodore."

"What way is that?"

"Completely. Unselfishly. Eternally. Why do you think I never remarried? I was young when Theodore died, and I did meet men in the subsequent years. At one point, the thought of remarriage actually crossed my mind." At Corinne's puzzled look, she went on. "You were too young to remember the man. He was a good man. He'd never been married before. He would have made a good father for you girls. At some point I realized that that was the main reason I was considering marrying him, but it would have been the worst reason to do so. You and Roxanne were destined to grow up and lead your own lives. I would have been left with a man who reminded me too often of what I'd lost when I lost Theodore."

"Oh, Gram, I'm sorry."

"For what? I had a wonderful husband, even if only for a short time. I'd like to hope that you'll have yours much longer. Has he asked you to marry him?"

It took Corinne a minute to shift gears. "Corey?"

"Is there any other man you'd consider marrying?"

"I haven't said that I'm considering marrying Corey."

"Has he asked?" Elizabeth repeated calmly.

For a minute Corinne considered lying, but only for a minute. While lying would hasten the end of the conversation, she wasn't sure she wanted it to end so quickly. She'd just seen a different side of her grandmother. She wanted to probe that side with regard to her own situation.

"Yes. He's asked."

"And you've turned him down. I'm glad."

Corinne was taken aback. "You *are*?" It seemed a direct contradiction to everything Elizabeth had said up to that point.

"Marriage is not a decision to be made lightly. You've never done things in haste, but when you finally decide to do them, you give them your all. I'm assuming that Corey loves you."

"He says he does."

"Still, you're not sure. May I ask why?"

"You can ask," Corinne said with an edgy chuckle. "I'm not sure I can answer."

"Try."

It took Corinne a minute to corral her thoughts. "I've told you some of the things, but there are others. Corey is the antithesis of the kind of man I'd imagined myself with. He has the reputation of a playboy, though he swears those days are over. He wheels and deals in the business world, though he swears that there's method to his madness. He invests in the stock market as though it were a game, though he swears that his instincts have never failed him."

"It sounds as though he swears quite a bit." Spoken sedately, but with twinkling eyes.

"I'm serious, Gram. He takes life so...lightly."

"Is that how he takes you?"

"No. At least, I don't think so. But can I depend on him?"

"Perhaps his lightness is a facade to cover up what may be a very serious approach to life."

"Perhaps. But there's more. He is unbelievably scatterbrained. I mean, I was there in his office when the bank called to say that his MasterCard was over its limit. He claimed he'd paid the bill right on time, and indeed he had. But he'd sent it in the same envelope with his check for American Express, which he discovered only after his poor secretary had spent four frantic hours on the phone."

"It was an honest mistake."

"Like mixing chicken with tartar sauce instead of mayonnaise to make chicken salad? He claimed the bottles looked alike."

Elizabeth cleared her throat. "It must have made an interesting chicken salad."

"And his contact lenses . . . The man called me in a panic one morning, saying that he'd be late picking me up because he'd lost one of them. He wore contacts so he wouldn't have to worry about misplacing glasses, and he'd lost one of the lenses!"

"I can see where he'd be alarmed. They're quite expensive, from what I've heard."

"They're insured, but that's beside the point. The point is that he inched his way through his bathroom looking for the lens, only to find that it was in his eye all along!"

"That was convenient."

"It was dumb!"

"Actually," Elizabeth decided, "it's rather sweet."

Corinne held her breath, then let it out with a sheepish smile. "I think you're right. The man is adorable at times, so much so that I could strangle him."

"It sounds to me as though you have a very nice blend of a man on your hands. He is a hard worker. He is devoted to you. He has his faults, but he does have spirit."

"Spirit can cause trouble."

"Not spirit that has a handle on it. Does your Corey have a handle on his spirit?"

"I don't know.... I think so...."

"Well, then." Elizabeth rose from her chair. "It's nearly my bedtime. I'll be going up—"

"But we haven't decided anything!" Corinne cried.

"We? It's not my decision to make, dear. You are the one who will be living with the man day after day, year after year, if you decide to marry him."

Corinne was out of her chair, following Elizabeth into the hall. "You can't go now, Gram."

"I can and I must. You have a lot of thinking to do, and I need my sleep."

"But Corey lives in South Carolina. If I marry him I'll be moving away." If anything would regain her grandmother's interest, she figured it would be that. Once again she was thwarted.

"There are airplanes," Elizabeth answered from midway up the stairs. "If Corey is going to have a hotel here in Baltimore, you'll be back to visit often enough."

"Won't you *miss* me?"

Elizabeth did stop then. Turning, she smiled very gently. ''You know that I'll miss you, Corinne. But I won't be around forever. I want you to have what I had—a husband who adores you. If your Corey does that, and if you can find it in your heart to see that his bills are paid properly, it seems to me that you have a foot up on the future. My missing you is a small price to pay for your happiness.'' Turning, she resumed her upward trek. ''Good night, dear.''

When Corinne returned to Hilton Head in the middle of June, she was armed with the questionnaire—professionally printed and ready for distribution—and the firm resolve to spend as much time as possible with Corey. She told herself that she simply needed to know him better if she was to make a rational decision regarding the future. But the truth was that when she was in his company, the pleasure of the moment was supreme.

To a certain extent, the discussion she'd had with her grandmother had been enlightening. Corinne had always assumed that Elizabeth would be as conservative with regard to a potential husband for Corinne as she was in her own, everyday life. Yet, it hadn't been so. Elizabeth had confidence in her; she didn't feel that Corinne was in danger of following in her mother's footsteps. Rather, her concern was that Corinne might miss out on something very special.

While being aware of her grandmother's feelings didn't erase her own hesitations, it helped put them in perspective. It was, therefore, with a more open-minded attitude that Corinne returned to Corey.

If her goal was to spend time with him, he accommodated her eagerly. During the brief waiting period after the first of the questionnaires had been distributed, he devoted himself to entertaining her. There were times when he needed to work, but he'd managed to clear his calendar of the most pressing business before she arrived, and what little needed to be done after, he insisted she do with him.

Then, there were the other times. They went shopping together—Corinne astounded herself by purchasing a slew of casual clothes, all of which she wore with pleasure. They spent the afternoon he'd promised exploring Savannah. They went fresh water fishing in a pond at Sea Pines and bird-watching along the lagoons. They went sailing and to the beach. And dancing. They went dancing night after night, and Corinne could only wonder what it was she'd feared. In Corey's arms she felt safe, sheltered and alive, so much so that the only problem she had was a growing inner frustration.

If the dreams she had at night and the daydreams she had when awake were any indication, she was slowly coming to accept the passionate side of her nature. Much as she loved them, the kisses Corey gave her each morning when he picked her up and each evening when he brought her back to the hotel left her far from sated. He was as well behaved as once upon a time she would have wanted, but once upon a time was just that. Now she wanted more. Unable yet to ask for it, she suffered in silence.

She wasn't the only one suffering. Though he never let it show, Corey was far from cool. Being with Corinne was heaven and hell, and while he wanted it to be heaven all the way, he was determined to let her call the shots.

In some ways the physical frustration eased when the completed questionnaires began to come in. Corinne was busy talking with respondents, and she and Corey had less time to spend together. In some ways, though, the frustration increased because during those less frequent times when they saw each other the attraction was more intense than ever.

Corey was nearly as amazed at his willpower as he was at the strength of the love behind it. It was actually in the name of the latter that he booked a suite in Atlanta for a weekend in the beginning of July. He was prepared for an argument from Corinne, though what he got was a pleasant surprise.

"Atlanta?" She smiled. "I've never really seen Atlanta."

"Then this will be the perfect chance," he said. He couldn't believe that she hadn't jumped on his mention of a suite, yet there was no prim face, no set jaw, no quelling glance. Actually, he hadn't seen any of those in a while. But then, he hadn't mentioned a *suite* before.

"I really shouldn't," she went on. Her sudden frown was blatantly phony. "There's so much to do here."

He wondered if she'd missed the implication of his booking a suite. Separate rooms, but connected. They'd be close. Very close. If she wanted, much could happen. "You've been working for nine days straight. You deserve some time off."

"Maybe I ought to fly back to Baltimore to check up on things there," she blurted, but the frown was gone and her eyes danced.

He could play the game, too. "Maybe you should."

"But I want to see Atlanta."

"Then I guess you'll have to come with me."

When she frowned again, he waited for the protest to begin in earnest. Instead, what she said after a short silence was, "I wonder if I have the right clothes. Maybe I could pick up something more dressy while we're there."

Corinne was excited. She knew that she loved Corey, that love had done nothing but grow during the past two weeks. Her life in Baltimore seemed light-years away, and she didn't miss it. She'd checked in with the office several times since she'd left. In each case she'd been happy to hang up the phone.

Corey had been the perfect companion. Day by day she was becoming more convinced of the truth of Elizabeth's words. He was a wonderful compromise—serious yet lighthearted, dedicated yet fun loving. He made her days pass with unbelievable speed and enjoyment, and he seemed to love her even without the sexual gratification she knew he sought.

She did know it. When they held each other and kissed, she felt his arousal. At those times she heard the roughness of his breathing and the low, involuntary moans of reluctance that accompanied their parting. She loved him all the more for his restraint, even if her own was sorely tested.

If the truth was told, regardless of what happened in Atlanta, she would still have questions. But Atlanta was necessary. Those questions that remained could be answered only after they'd explored the limits of their passion together, which was why Corinne made a conscious decision to make love with Corey.

# 8

Making a conscious decision was one thing, putting it into effect quite another. Corinne made a quick trip to the drugstore, determined that she wouldn't be so irresponsible as to overlook birth control. She'd felt self-conscious poring over the offerings, but that had actually been the easy part.

She had never seen herself as a seductress, much less acted like one. When she tried to plan how she would lure Corey, she was stymied. Come-hither looks weren't her style, any more than were deliberate hand stroking and thigh brushing. Always when she'd come to life in his arms, she'd been acting instinctively, not rationally. Even now, as they sat on the airplane en route to Atlanta, that visceral part of her was reacting to his size, his closeness, his scent. To put her feelings into words and action, though, was beyond her. Clear-mindedly plotting out passion seemed both inappropriate and contradictory.

But she did want to make love with him. The question was how to make him aware of it and, more importantly, how to let him know that she didn't want him to apply the brakes.

Unfortunately, she had no answers. As a result, the closer they came to Atlanta, the more nervous she grew.

Corey was well aware of it. He was aware of the fact that she wouldn't look him in the eye and that she seemed increasingly preoccupied. He saw the way her fingers clenched around the strap of her purse and the way she fumbled through the airline magazine without reading a page. He assumed that she was having her doubts about the wisdom of sharing a suite, and though he didn't want to, he was prepared to exert the same self-control he had practiced so frequently during the past weeks.

She was visibly uncomfortable when they checked into the hotel in Atlanta, even more so when the bellboy showed them to their rooms. Once they were alone, Corey watched her walk awkwardly through the suite, heard the tightness in her voice when she praised its lavishness.

He didn't want praise for what simple money could buy, he wanted Corinne without the tight voice, awkward walk and visible discomfort. He wanted the Corinne he knew and loved, the one who opened only for him, the one who relaxed and enjoyed herself and trusted that he wouldn't lead her astray. He decided to speak up, to confront her, to make her air what was on her mind so that he could put her worries to rest.

She was at the window, staring out over Peachtree Center far below, when he came up behind her. He didn't come close, certainly not close enough to touch her, and there was nothing seductive about his voice when he spoke. It was quiet, tight in its own way.

"Is everything okay?"

Her voice had a forced brightness, and she didn't turn. "It's lovely here, thank you."

"Are *you* okay?"

"Couldn't be better."

"Something's bothering you."

"No, no. Everything's fine."

"Are you sorry you came?"

"Of course not. Why would you think that?"

"You seem tense." When she didn't answer, he prodded. "Tell me what you're thinking."

"It's a lovely view from here."

"Tell me what you're really thinking."

"Just that."

"Turn around and say it to my face."

She hesitated. Slowly she turned. Even more slowly she raised her eyes to his.

His heart sank. There was no way he could miss the sadness, the regret, the confusion. Alan had warned him; a thirty-year-old virgin was so for a reason. Corey had been arrogant enough to think he could overcome any and all obstacles. Now he wasn't so sure.

He spoke quickly, only then aware of how frightened he was of losing everything Corinne was, just for the sake of sex. "Listen, Cori. There's nothing to be upset about. Just because I booked us a suite doesn't mean that I've assumed we'd sleep together. There are two bedrooms. Nothing has to happen here that you don't want."

"But I—"

"We can go out for lunch, then take a walk around the city. We can do some shopping, maybe go to a movie or a show. We can go to the amusement park if you want."

"I'd like that, but—"

"Maybe you're tired. If you want to rest, I swear I won't go near your room."

"Corey, I—"

"I love you, Corinne," he said more softly. He raised his hand to her cheek, lightly touching her skin. "I want you to be happy. That means more to me than anything else right now. I'm willing to wait for anything more until you're sure about your feelings."

"I am," she breathed, frustrated both by the fact that he hadn't let her get a word in edgewise and, in a different way, by the simple fact of his nearness. She wanted to reach out but she felt shy.

"You are?" he asked. His voice was tight again. "You want me to get lost."

She shook her head.

"Then what?"

"I love you."

His eyes widened. "You ... do?"

She nodded.

"You do love me?" he asked, afraid to believe it.

"Very much."

He gave a loud whoop of joy and slid his hand around the back of her neck. "Then what's the problem? We can go out and have a wonderful time—"

"I don't want to go out. I want to stay here. With you."

She'd spoken so softly and calmly that Corey might have missed her implication if he hadn't seen the way her breasts were rising and falling with the shallow breaths she took and the way her cheeks had grown pink. He felt as though he'd been hit by a sledgehammer.

She spoke again before he'd quite recovered. "I'm sorry. I don't know how to say it. I haven't had much experience."

"You said it—" he paused to clear his throat "—very well."

Corinne searched his eyes for the smokiness of passion and saw nothing but astonishment. She broke away from him and covered her face. "I shouldn't have said it. I'm not good at this. I can't expect you to be turned on and off like a light."

Corey pried her hands from her face. "I'm never turned off," he said with wonder. "Never with you. It's just that I'm amazed. I've waited so long, wanted so badly to hear you say that you love me, and to have you say you want me in the same breath...."

"I'm sorry."

"Don't be sorry. Corinne—" he pulled her against him "—don't ever be sorry for that. I love you so much. I don't want you to be sorry for anything, ever."

"My timing is off," she whispered against his shirt. "I know what I want and I've thought it all out, but my timing is off."

"Not for me it isn't." One breath of her lemony scent would have done it, even if the feel of her small, perfectly formed body hadn't. "I want you, Cori. I always have. I always will."

"That's what I have to know," came her muffled assertion.

"Haven't I said it before?"

"Saying it isn't enough. I need to know."

Corey heard something in her voice that puzzled him. He held her back and looked down at her. "What is it, exactly, that you need to know?"

"I need to know that you'll still want me after we've made love."

"Of course, I—"

"I need to know that I'll still want you."

He understood then. She was thinking of her parents, who'd never been satisfied with one partner alone. "You're not like them."

"But I need to know," she cried. "Don't you see? I can't commit myself to you unless I do. It wouldn't be fair."

"I have no doubts," he said with confidence.

"Then show me. Show me, Corey. Please?"

It occurred to Corey just then that in the months he'd known Corinne she'd asked very little of him. She was an independent soul, self-contained in many ways. When she asked something she did it from the heart.

With a low moan of long-suppressed desire, he lowered his head and took her lips in a kiss that spoke of his love and his passion as no words could have ever done. They were both slightly breathless when at last he drew away. Again he looked down at her, this time with the smoky gaze she'd been wanting, but with caution, as well.

"We could do a little something outside, then come back here later."

She shook her head.

"We could order up a bottle of wine or champagne or something."

"No," she whispered. "I want to do it now."

"Are you sure? Really sure, sweetheart?"

"I'm really sure."

Moaning again, he hugged her tightly, then, easing her to his side, led her toward the larger of the two bedrooms. Beneath his arm, against his side, he felt her trembling.

"Are you frightened?"

"A little."

"Me, too."

"But you've done this before."

"Never with a woman I loved."

They stopped by the bed. He released her to toss back the spread and blanket. "I haven't, Corey," she said nervously. "I haven't done it with anyone before."

He turned to find her knotting her hands at her waist. "I know," he said, smiling gently as he took her hands in his. "That's one of the things that makes you so special."

"I won't know what to do."

"You'll know."

"If I do something wrong, will you tell me?"

"You won't do anything wrong."

"How can you be so sure?"

"Because you have what it takes inside. You've always had it. I've never needed to instruct you before. Sometimes you've been a step ahead of me."

"That's when I'm not thinking."

"No one says you have to think now."

"But I want to. I want to know what's happening."

"Then I'll tell you. Sound fair?"

She nodded.

His eyes were warm, loving her features with nothing but a visual caress. "Should I draw the drapes?"

"No," she whispered. "I want to see."

"You won't be shocked?" There was a twinkle in his eye. He wanted to see, too, but he'd expected her to feel shy at first.

"I want to see," she repeated in that same soulful whisper.

"Okay," he murmured, and drew her down to sit facing him on the bed. Cradling her face in his hands, he kissed her again, starting slowly, deepening it when he felt her response. It occurred to him, as his tongue slid into her mouth, that it wasn't going to be easy taking things slow. Simply kissing her made his body throb. Of course, it wasn't only the kiss, he knew, but the prospect of what was to come. He imagined her body naked, his body naked, their stomachs rubbing, their legs intertwining. He imagined being sheathed by her warmth—then he stopped his imagining because he was already far too hard.

Lips still clinging to hers, he set shaky fingers to work on the buttons of his shirt. When he was done he let the shirt hang open. "Touch me, Cori." His voice was husky. "I've waited so long to feel your hands on me."

Corinne, who'd lost herself completely in his kiss, forced her eyes open. They grew wider when they saw the flesh he'd bared. It was bronzed and firm, softened by a carpet of mahogany-colored hair. She'd seen him shirtless before, when they'd gone to the beach, but it was different now, more intimate. She was free to touch him, as she hadn't been then. Taking a tremulous breath, she put her fingertips on his chest. Within seconds she'd flattened her palm and begun to move it around.

"Tell me what you feel," Corey whispered. His eyes were glued to her face, taking in the expression of awe she wore.

"I feel...you feel warm. Hard, solid, but soft. The hair..." Mesmerized, she watched that hair curl between her splayed fingers. It was thicker at spots; she explored those, working through the mat on his upper chest, following a downward, narrowing path. It was thinner at spots; she let her other hand join its mate to spread over his rib cage, then upward, where small, flat nipples lay.

Those nipples didn't remain flat for long but came to quick attention under the innocent tutelage of her fingers. Corey closed his eyes against the pleasure that flooded him. He bit his lip and fought for control.

"That feels . . . ahhh, good."

Corinne was so engrossed in what she was doing that she barely heard his words. Her hands were moving more broadly, easing aside his shirt as they shaped the muscled swell of his breast.

"You're beautifully made," she whispered. The words seemed so inadequate, given the appreciation she felt, that she lowered her head and kissed his chest. It was one way to worship him, and the gratification she found in it was immense. Her mouth pressed damply against his skin, lips stroking him as she inched from one side to another.

His hands suddenly dove into her hair. His voice came from farther away, as well it should have, for his head was thrown back. "Cori, oh Lord, Cori...I need more . . . more." Bringing his head forward, he tipped hers up to meet it. The kiss he gave her was fierce and telling. When he looked at her again, his green eyes were dusky. "Touch me more," he whispered hoarsely. "Lower."

Corinne was in a dreamlike state. The raw, musky scent of him drugged her. The heat of his body compounded that of her own. He was saying something, suggesting something. She struggled to clear her head. "It's so hard to . . . concentrate . . . you feel so good."

He choked out a chuckle. "Tell me about it, and we've barely begun. Do you really expect to keep sane?"

She wanted to. She wanted to know what she was doing and how it affected him. With a tiny shake to clear her head, she whispered, "Yes."

"Is that no," he asked, referring to the headshake, "or yes?"

"Yes," she said more clearly.

Before she could get another word out, he'd shifted her onto his lap. The added height of his thigh brought her up to eye level with him. He promptly lowered his head and began to nuzzle her neck. "Now touch," he commanded.

She was more than willing to comply but from this new angle the first thing she wanted to do was to remove his shirt completely. She wanted free access not only to his chest but to his shoulders and back, as well.

The shirt fell to the bed and for a minute all she could do was marvel at what she'd uncovered. Then she began to touch him in gentle sweeps that gradually moved from his back to his front and wandered lower. His flesh was new but familiar and dear. Her fingers felt right against it, even as they ventured into the narrow space at his waistband that opened when he sucked in his breath.

"What do you feel?" she whispered.

"Fire!" His head dipped lower, mouth opening against her breast. He closed it, raking his teeth across her nipple. Even through the fabric of her tunic top and bra, she felt the heat and gasped.

She was aware, and she was feeling it. She was analyzing passion, taking it apart element by element, trying to understand its force. "The heat goes deeper and deeper," she breathed. "It's like an insatiable hunger...." Her hand fell lower over his slacks, coming to rest against the hard rod behind his zipper. Her fingers measured it. The heel of her hand tested its strength. Then her whole hand spread and loosely cupped the heaviness between his legs.

Corey's breath came out in an agonized moan.

Her hand froze. "I hurt you."

He gave an embarrassed half laugh. "No. No. The reverse. Do it again."

Her cheek rubbed back and forth against his thick auburn hair, while her hand stroked and squeezed. Passion was the swelling of flesh and its throbbing— his sex at her caress, her breast at his suckling. She tried to find something wrong with what either of them were doing but could conclude that the only thing wrong was that it wasn't enough.

Without conscious analysis Corey reached the same decision. "Let's take this off," he growled, tugging at her tunic and whipping it over her head. His mouth was back, then, lips and tongue coaxing her strapless bra down inch by inch until the rosy crest of her breast appeared. "Ahhh, sweet..." He sighed. He enveloped her nipple and drew on it deeply.

She cried out then, pressing her legs together against the shaft of fire that seared her there. Her hand had gone still against him; for a minute she simply couldn't think.

"I want you naked," Corey whispered. "Now." Shifting her back to the bed, he unhooked her bra and cast it aside, taking a moment to adore her breasts with his eyes before he was tugging her pants and panties down her legs.

When she wore nothing but the midday sun that filtered in through the large picture window, he came down on one knee on the bed. His gaze started at her toes, worked its way up her legs to the dark triangle at their apex, then upward, over her flat belly and rib cage to her breasts, and finally to her face. Unable to speak, he simply shook his head in wonder. Then he lifted her and crushed her against him.

"What are you thinking?" she asked in a whisper.

It was a minute before he was able to make a sound. Even then his voice was strangled. "I'm thinking…that I've never seen anything…as beautiful, and that I want you to…be mine more than I've wanted anything in my life."

Corinne smiled against his chest. His words were ample reward for the effort it had taken not to move beneath his examination.

"Do you feel shy?" he asked, reading her mind.

"A little. And proud." Her voice was barely more than a breath. "I've never felt proud like this. One part of me wanted to cover up, but the other part wanted you to see. Wants you to see. Wants you to touch. Wants…" Her hands shimmied between their bodies and fumbled blindly with the fastener of his pants. "Wants to see you, too."

"Oh Lord," he groaned. Laying her down, he began to tear at his pants. He didn't take his eyes from her face, and when he was naked, he came to her quickly. His arms were straight, his weight on the heels of the hands by her hips as he searched her gaze. "I don't want to frighten you."

"I'm not frightened," she whispered, realizing that she no longer was. There was no room for fear when desire clogged the mind. Desire, and wonder, and appreciation. She'd never seen anything as artistically perfect as Corey's maleness. Coming up on an elbow, she looked down his body. She put a hand on his shoulder, drew it over his chest, then his waist and hip.

When she raised her eyes she was, as Corey had been moments before, without words.

Not so Corey. He hadn't withstood Corinne's examination half as stoically as she had. That part of him over which he had little control had reached a state of painful distension. He knew that he wouldn't be able to hold back much longer, but he also remembered his promise to tell her what was happening.

"I'm going to kiss you again," he said, and did. He made love to her mouth as he'd soon do to her body. "And touch you, this time not only with my hands, but the rest of me." He did that, too, moving over her, shifting back and forth, stoking her fire and his own with the combustible force of male against female from shoulders to toes. All the while his hands journeyed from one erotic spot to another, and his tongue taunted hers to distraction.

Corinne tried to take in all that was happening, but there was simply too much. She wanted to concentrate on the feel of his chest against hers, but her attention was diverted by the glide of his hair-roughened thighs, then the touch of his hand drawing her knee up, then the jutting shaft against her belly.

When Corey lowered his hand to the spot between her legs that was most sensitive and needy, she couldn't think of anything but the flames. She cried out his name and strained against those fingers that were opening her, finding her warmth and her wetness.

It was the end of restraint for them both. Passion was the need to become one in the most elemental way. Positioning himself over her, Corey wound his fingers through hers and anchored them by her shoulders. "Look at me," he whispered, and waited until she'd opened her eyes. He knew that the agony he saw there was reflected in his own gaze. It was the agony of desire and was echoed by the ache in his voice. "I'm going to love you now. I need to be inside. It may hurt at first, but I'll be quick. Okay?"

*I love you.* The words were mouthed but he heard each one. As he repeated them in kind, he gave a powerful thrust forward.

They both cried out then, but the pain was only at the beauty of the union.

"Corey . . . so full . . ."

"Tight . . . wonderful . . . ahhhh . . ." Carefully he withdrew, then more slowly pressed forward. He'd never felt so neatly sheathed, so loved. Stroking gently, he repeated the motion. When she sighed this time she raised her knees and urged him deeper.

There were no more words. Passion was an eddy of overwhelming feelings and sensations. Corinne hadn't known, or she'd never have assumed she could be rational to the end. Passion was love, and love was Corey. Instinct was the primal force that bound the three in a never-ending circle.

Corey set the rhythm; Corinne met it, hastened it. The fire burned ever brighter and deeper until it exploded in multiple bursts of blinding light, leaving them both gasping and panting, clinging to each other, then collapsing onto the bed in a heap of sweat-slick arms, legs and torsos.

The heap took organized form when, at long last, Corey mustered the strength to slip to her side and draw her into the haven of his arms. It was later yet before he was able to speak. With a not quite steady hand he brushed damp spikes of hair from her forehead.

"I've been bewitched," he said softly, smiling when she opened her eyes.

"Is that good or bad?"

"Good and bad." When her brow furrowed lightly, his smile broadened. He drew his finger across the creases, but it was his words that erased them. "Good, because I've never been so... touched by anything in my life. Bad, because you've ruined me. I'll never be satisfied with anything less."

"I hope not."

"I know not."

The beginnings of a lazy smile played with her lips. "When I stop and think of all we've missed... We could have done that in the gazebo, or on the boat...."

"Nuh-uh. It wouldn't have been the same then. You didn't know you loved me. That's what's made it so special now."

Still smiling, Corinne closed her eyes, took a deep, shuddering breath and wrapped herself more closely around Corcy. "I do love you," she whispered, and at the moment she didn't care what the future held. The present was far too lovely to allow the intrusion of fear and worry.

Corey's heart was as full as his body was depleted. The only thing that would have made his happiness perfect would have been her agreement to marry him. But he didn't want to mention marriage. Somewhere deep inside, he knew that she still needed time. He'd been patient, and she'd come to him physically. He had to believe that if he was patient on the issue of marriage, one day she would come to him in that way, too.

The dream brought a hum of satisfaction from his throat. He nestled her closer, rubbing his chin over the top of her head. "I love your hair. You don't need long curls to hide behind."

"I couldn't have curls if I tried. This stuff is stick straight."

"But I love it that way. It always smells so good." He inhaled and smiled. "Lemon turns me on."

She tipped her head back. "What else turns you on?"

"Small women with slender legs, full breasts and bottoms that—turn over. I wanna see."

"I can't move."

"Then I'll feel." His hand settled on her fanny, moved to the left, then the right, then up and down.

She drew in her breath. She'd never dreamed she had so many erogenous zones, but something was definitely stirring inside. Or was it the mere touch of his hands? Or the scent of his body, more earthy now? Or the sturdiness of his muscled frame flexing and swelling against her?

"Corey?"

He cleared his throat, but his voice came out thicker anyway. "Compactly rounded bottoms. They turn me on."

"Me, too."

"Mine isn't as round as yours."

"No?" She made a tactile examination, never once taking her eyes from his. "You're right. It's tighter. But it turns me on anyway."

Their lips met gently.

"I think we should get up," he whispered.

"Nooooo. Not yet."

"If we stay like this, I'm gonna take you again."

"Okay."

"It's not. You'll be sore."

"I don't feel sore."

"I think," he said, forcing himself to sit up, "that a nice warm bath would be just what the doctor ordered."

She tried to pull him back, but his body was unyielding. "I don't want a bath right now."

"I'll take one with you."

Second to making love again, that thought was appealing. "You will?"

He scooped her into his arms and left the bed. "Did you think I'd let you go so quick?" He was walking toward the bathroom. "We'll take a nice warm bath, get dressed, then explore the city."

Her arms were around his neck. "We'll make love later?"

"If you want."

"I want now."

Sighing, he set her on her feet by the huge tub. "Corinne," he said sternly, "I am trying to do what's best for you. Don't argue."

Her gaze dropped from his face to the column of his neck, then down over his chest, along the narrowing line of hair past his waist to that spot where the hair thickened again. Something else had thickened.

"Yes, I want you," he grumbled, "but I think we ought to wait. Hell, Cori, I could take you over and over all day, I'm that hungry for you." He was standing with his hands low on his hips, not daring to touch her, but his voice softened. "I'll always be hungry for you. That won't change. But I refuse to let you think that that's all I want from you, because it isn't. What I want right now is to take a bath with you. Then I want to walk through the streets and show you off. Then I want to take you to lunch, maybe do some shopping, maybe stop somewhere else or just walk more. I want—'' he grinned crookedly ''—to see you dressed and know that I'm the only man to know what's underneath.''

Her own lips twitched. ''You do?''

''I do.'' Afraid to trust himself further, he bent and turned on the water.

She ran a hand down his spine. His back was perfect—symmetrical laterally, tapering vertically from broad shoulders to narrow hips. His skin was smooth, marred only by a small birthmark just above his waist. She touched it lightly.

Corey straightened with a shiver of awareness. He glared at her for a minute, then lowered his head and shook it. From that position he looked up at her. Before she could analyze his intent, he'd swept her into his arms, stepped into the tub and knelt, spreading her legs over his thighs.

''You're impossible,'' he breathed, then he kissed her hard.

She loved the hardness. She loved the way his muscles had begun to quiver. And she loved the way his sex pressed against that spot that cried so for his possession.

His fingers did the possessing first, gently urging warm water over her, soothing her, tenderly stroking the tiny nub that was so very sensitive. When he cupped her bottom and brought her forward, the ease of his entry astonished him. Embedded deeply, he held her still.

''You're something else,'' he breathed, smiling down at her. He dropped his gaze to the point of their joining, laid his thumb there and did something that made her gasp. Then he looked up into an expression so open that his heart swelled. "You're not modest."

"Not with you." It was hard to think with what he was doing to her, but some things needed little thought. "You make everything seem so right."

"It is, Cori. Everything *is* right."

She didn't try to think beyond that, because Corey started to move inside her and the rush for fulfillment took over. At some point, he remembered to turn off the water, though it was doubtful she would have known it if she had been drowning. When a forceful climax shook her, followed quickly by Corey's, she suffered the little death that not long ago she would have thought impossible.

Not long ago she'd thought many things were impossible. She'd thought herself incapable of opening to a man. She'd thought herself incapable of loving one deeply. She'd wanted to think that she was incapable of feeling mindless rapture, but Corey had shown her differently. All that was left was for him to show her—and for her to show herself—that what was indeed possible was only so between the two of them.

Corey had no way of knowing that as they ambled through Atlanta later that afternoon, Corinne was on the lookout for men. She saw a dashing dark-haired businessman, alone with his newspaper in the restaurant at which they stopped for lunch. She saw an adorable sandy-haired intellectual type in the bookstore where they stopped to browse. She saw a positively gorgeous, scantily clad runner lope past the window of the boutique where she bought a beautiful evening dress.

None of the three did the slightest thing to her insides, yet all she had to do was to look at Corey's smiling face and those insides crinkled. Her fingers itched when her gaze fell on his thick, auburn hair. Her knees weakened when she took in the whole of his tall, lean frame.

She decided that Corey Haraden was simply too much of a man to permit thought of any other when she was in his presence. And with that decision made, she had eyes only for him for the rest of the weekend.

They did all the things Corey had suggested and more. But if Corinne thought she'd be tired when they returned to their suite, she was mistaken. They made love when they came back to change for dinner, then, repeatedly, throughout the night. They had breakfast in bed on Sunday morning, then promptly devoured each other. They even returned for a quickie before they packed their things, then unpacked as quickly when, on the spur of the moment, they decided to stay the extra night and fly to Savannah on Monday morning.

It was after they'd landed there, when they were driving to the island, that Corey brought her hand to his lips.

"I know what you're thinking," he said. He kissed her knuckles lightly. "You're thinking that once we get back to the island things will be different. They won't be, Cori."

That was exactly what she'd been thinking, fearing. She wished she could be as certain as he was. "It's been such a wonderful two days. I wish they didn't have to end."

"They don't...at least, not in essence. We both have work to do, but that doesn't mean that we can't be together in our free time."

"Do you want that?"

He nipped at one of her fingers. "Are you kidding?"

"Aren't you looking forward, even a tiny bit, to having a breather?"

"At the office? No way. The breather I get will be taking you home with me each night."

"Uh...Corey..."

"You're moving in with me."

"I can't do that. It'd look awful."

"No, it would not, and even if it did, I don't give a damn. I want you with me."

"You could come to my suite."

"I want you at my home."

"It'll be easier for me to work at the hotel if I'm staying there."

"I'll drive you there in the morning and drive you home at night. I'll leave a car at your disposal so you can have all the mobility you need during the day." His fingers tightened around hers. "Hell, Cori, you were planning to go back to Baltimore at the end of the week, anyway. I want to make the most out of the time we have left."

"I'll be back. That was the plan."

"And when you come back, I want you staying with me. I will not share you," he stated emphatically. "I mean it."

Corinne's heart soared to hear him say it, and say it with such determination. It occurred to her that he might feel differently in a week, a month, a year.... But she knew that only time would tell that. She could worry herself sick, and the only thing she'd accomplish would be to spoil the time they had together. She didn't want to do that.

"So you really think I should live with you?"

"Yes."

"You don't think that the others who went in with you on the project will wonder if they were railroaded?"

"They'll get their survey done, and it'll be done well. They won't have any complaints. If anything, they'll be relieved to know that their secretaries and administrative assistants aren't in danger anymore." He felt her fingers twitch and shot her a glance. "Uh-uh. Don't do that. I can't change what I was before I met you."

"I know," she said softly.

"I'm not one bit sorry those days are over."

"Are you sure?"

"Corinne, I've asked you to marry me. Doesn't that say something? Uh, don't even bother to answer that, because you'll be thinking of your parents. I'm not like them. One of the reasons I've waited so long to marry is that I've never met a woman I could think of forever with. When I marry it'll be for good. That's how it was with my parents. That's how it will be for me." He took a quick breath. "But since you don't want to talk marriage yet, and I don't want to push you, I'm asking you to live with me ... at least during the time you're here. And mind you—" he was getting worked up "—I don't relish the idea of your going back to Baltimore at all. I know you have to. Your job is there, and your grandmother. But if I had my way, you'd move lock, stock and barrel down here.

Hell, if I had my way, we'd be making wedding plans right now!''

He worked her knuckles around his mouth, giving himself time to calm down. "So. I'm asking you to live with me." He cast her a coaxing look. "I've never asked a woman to live with me before."

"You haven't?" she asked, but there was a hint of teasing in her voice.

"No, ma'am, so you'd better consider it."

"You're really a slob." She'd had the dubious pleasure of being at his house one morning before Jontelle had arrived. Newspapers were strewed about, dirty glasses stood on the counter, mail was scattered over the kitchen table, clothes over the bedroom. It had amazed her that one man could make such a mess in such a short time, particularly given the fact he'd been out of the house—with her—the evening before.

"You can reform me."

"I'm not sure that's possible."

"Then don't reform me, but you're moving in anyway."

"You sleep on the left side of the bed."

"So?"

"So do I."

"You didn't last night, or the night before."

"That's because I didn't have the strength to move either me *or* you."

He gnawed comically on her hand. "I'll sleep on the right once you move in with me."

"Corey—"

"No more arguments, Corinne. I say you're living with me, and Cardinal Rule nawmnga gueeeyyy—"

She'd put her finger into his mouth.

"All I was going to say," she whispered, leaning close, "is that it might be nice some night to make love on your patio...."

They made love on his patio, in his kitchen, in the bathroom, the den and, of course, the bedroom. The old Corinne would have been appalled; the new Corinne accepted the passion within her and was almost defiantly pushing it to its limits. The only problem was that there seemed to be no limits at all. The mere sight of Corey excited her. His slightest touch aroused her. She saw no sign that her interest in Corey, or his in her, was weakening.

She looked at other men. In the course of her work, she had occasion to interact with many. She tried to find things about them that were appealing. She dared herself to find them exciting.

She failed.

At the end of the week, she returned to Baltimore. Leaving Corey was hard to do, but it was necessary. He had business trips to take, and she had work to do in the office. She wanted to see her grandmother and catch up on things around the house. Most importantly, she had to know what would happen when miles separated Corey and her.

What happened was that she missed him desperately. When she looked at another man, she saw Corey. When she tried to analyze that man, feature by feature, she turned away in disinterest long before she was done.

Life with her grandmother seemed suddenly far too regimented, the old Victorian house far too neat. When she was at work she had half an eye on the door, looking, waiting, hoping that Corey would pop in.

He didn't, of course. Regardless of where he was, he called her each night wanting to know about her day, wanting to tell her about his and that he loved her. She began to count the days, then hours until she'd return to him, and when the last minute came, then went, she ran into his arms without the slightest care for where they were or who could see.

Corey's welcome was everything she'd dreamed. His delight was boundless. He couldn't stop grinning, or touching, or even just looking. It had never occurred to him that she wouldn't return; he had the faith that she lacked in herself.

That faith, though, wasn't as lacking as it had once been. As the days passed, Corinne was beginning to think that maybe, maybe it all just might work. They'd been separated for a week, during which time each had had opportunity to seek out others, yet neither had. If anything, the time apart had increased their need for each other. Their relationship seemed deeper, as though its roots had grown and spread, producing that much stronger a foundation for their love.

Time was all Corinne needed. She told Corey as much each time he mentioned marriage, which he did whenever he dared. Strangely, she didn't mind his raising the issue. She felt badly putting him off, but she would have felt worse if he'd seemed content with their live-in arrangement. Marriage carried with it a sense of permanency. Assuming the right kind of marriage, permanency was exactly what she wanted.

There was permanency in other relationships, as well, though. A week into her latest trip to Hilton

Head, Corinne received a call from her grandmother to say that Roxanne had disappeared. Corinne had no choice but to pack her bags and take the first plane north.

# 9

Corey insisted on flying to New York with her.

"You have so much to do here," she protested. As it was, she knew that he was purposely staying put while she was at Hilton Head, which meant that he was juggling things long-distance that normally he would have done in person.

He continued to throw clothes haphazardly into a bag. "Anything that can't wait, I can handle by phone. This is important."

"But you've never even *met* my sister."

"She's your sister. That's the only thing that counts."

"Corey, are you sure? I hate imposing on you this way."

"Cori, I'm sure, and it's not like you asked me to come. I asked myself. I'm coming."

"But—"

"Cardinal Rule Number Fourteen—"

"I know, I know," she cried in a voice an octave above normal, then made a face at his bag. "You're making a mess of those clothes. They'll be unwearable by the time we reach New York." She set about straightening them, grateful for the diversion. She was feeling slightly frantic about Roxanne and overwhelmingly relieved that Corey *was* coming. It was all she could do not to cry.

When they finally made it onto the plane and took off, she reached for his hand. "Thank you. I feel better knowing you're here."

"Which isn't saying a helluva lot right now. You're feeling pretty low."

She raised guilt-ridden eyes to his. "She cried out to me in one letter after another. I talked with her on the phone, but I should have gone to see her. I didn't do enough."

"You've been busy."

"But she's my sister."

"She's a big girl. She's married, and a mother. You can't be her keeper, Cori. You did what you could."

Corinne was shaking her head, not so much in contradiction as in disbelief. "How could she *leave* that way? I mean, she was upset with Frank, but Jeffrey... How could she have left *him*?"

"Did Frank say what she wrote in her note?"

"Just that she needed to fly. I can't even believe she used that expression. It's something mother would say."

"Do you think Roxanne's gone to see her?"

"Mother? Not unless Rox has truly cracked up. Cerise is a free spirit. She hasn't ever wanted any part of her daughters." Her tone had hardened. "I don't even want to have to call her and ask, not that I'd know where to reach her anyway."

"Frank must be calling around."

"I'd think so, but he sounded really shaken. I've never heard him like that. I have a feeling he's pacing the floor, not knowing quite what to do for the first time in his life."

She was right. Frank was uncharacteristically un-raveled. His relief at seeing Corey and her was nearly as great as it would have been had Roxanne herself walked through the door.

Roxanne didn't walk through the door, of course. Between the three of them they phoned every friend she had. No one had seen or heard from her.

They considered the possibility of foul play, then ruled it out based on the note she'd left. They de-bated calling the police, but vetoed that idea for the same reason; the police would have little interest in a case where a wife had deserted her husband and child of her own free will. They did call Alex in Paris—ac-tually, Corey did, claiming to be an old friend of Roxanne's who was trying to reach her. Alex simply gave him Frank's address.

Putting their heads together, they tried to figure out where she would have gone. She'd left the car. It was possible that she was still in Manhattan, in a hotel un-der an assumed name. Or she might have flown out of the city, or taken a train or a bus. If any of those were the case, it would take an expert to find her.

So they set out to hire a private investigator. Again, it was Corey who took the initiative. After several calls to associates of his in the city, he came up with the name of a reputable woman, who graciously met with them that night. They told her as much as they could about Roxanne—her personal style, likes and dis-likes. Frank gave her several pictures, plus names of the banks from which she might have withdrawn money and credit card information.

By midmorning the next day, the investigator learned that Roxanne had withdrawn a small sum from her personal bank account on the day she'd left.

She had also charged a plane ticket to Chicago. It was a start.

For the rest of that day Corinne, Corey and Frank remained close by the phone in the Shiltons' penthouse apartment. They reasoned that Roxanne's having charged the plane ticket was a good sign; she was leaving a trail. They also understood that time was of the essence; even the most carefully laid bread crumbs could be scattered by the wind, eaten by animals or simply dissolved into the earth by the rain.

Frank did his share of pacing the floor. He also talked. He clearly blamed himself for what had happened, admitting to having been blind to Roxanne's needs and deaf to her subtle pleas. When Corinne told him of the letters Roxanne had sent her, he was even more distraught. He should have seen, should have heard, should have done something, he cried. He admitted to having taken his wife for granted and seemed genuinely angry with himself—just as he seemed genuinely grieved that Roxanne had left and genuinely fearful for her well-being.

He wasn't much help with Jeffrey. Corinne and Corey, with the help of the nanny, saw that the child's day was as normal as possible. When he asked for his mother they explained that she'd taken a trip and that she would be back. They could only pray that they wouldn't be proved wrong.

In one rare moment when they were alone, Corinne turned to Corey. "I've always feared this would happen," she whispered. "There's something in the genes. I swear there is."

Corey put his arm around her. He knew how upset she was and would have done anything in his power to ease her mind. "Not in the genes, sweetheart. In the mind. In Roxanne's case, if there is any resemblance to your parents it's probably a matter of the power of suggestion. Roxanne wanted to get Frank's attention. When she couldn't do it by conventional means, she followed the only other example she knew.''

''Do you think she did it consciously?''

''From what you've said, she's a bright woman. She may have acted in the extreme in trying to rouse Frank, but chances are that was exactly what she intended. As for specifically setting out to take a page from your parents' book—'' He shrugged. ''Who knows?''

Corinne was making silent analogies between her fears about herself and what Roxanne had done. ''What do you think she's looking for?''

''Maybe nothing. She may simply want Frank to have to do the looking.''

''She may be looking for someone who will shower her with attention. Or sex. Maybe she's looking for that.''

''I don't think so,'' came a deep voice behind them. They whirled to find Frank beneath the living room archway.

Corinne was instantly appalled. ''I'm sorry, Frank. I didn't mean to suggest—''

His upheld hand cut her off. ''No harm done, Cori. You have a right to suggest anything you want. Roxanne is your sister, and obviously I haven't done a very good job of taking care of her. But one thing I can tell you. We've never had a problem in bed. I may be an old fuddy-duddy about some things, and I've already admitted that I've had blinders on with regard to a good many others, but sex doesn't fall under either category.'' He didn't appear to be embarrassed. He was stating a fact. "Did Roxanne ever complain about that in her letters?"

"No."

"I can understand why not. Sex was the one way we ever truly communicated." He rubbed the back of his neck. "If it weren't so, she might have run off a long time ago." Wearing a pained expression, he left the room.

For a long time Corinne said nothing. Then she turned into Corey and wrapped her arms tightly around him. "The torment. That's what I fear. Frank is an adult. He'll learn to cope in time. But Jeffrey... There's only so long that he'll believe his mother's on a trip, and if she doesn't come back—"

"She will," Corey vowed. "She will. Y'know, in some ways you have to be grateful that your parents were never around. Their example would have been much stronger if they'd been running around under your noses. Look at it this way. The prime examples in Roxanne's life and yours were set by your grandmother. Her values were the ones you were both raised on. Those values will bring Roxanne back."

"They didn't bring my mother back."

"No, but your mother was young and impressionable when she left, and she had Alex to give her encouragement. Roxanne has no one like that. Frank is levelheaded and down to earth, and he wants her back. Maybe that's what this whole thing's about—her way of finding out exactly how much Frank does care. Besides, you said yourself that she adores Jeffrey and that she wants to take care of him. Does that sound like your mother?"

"No. Oh, Corey, I hope you're right. For all our sakes, I hope you're right."

He was, but not until after they'd all gone through the hell of thinking the opposite. Late that afternoon the investigator called to say that Roxanne had flown from Chicago to Las Vegas, but that the trail had temporarily gone dead there.

Corinne fidgeted in Corey's arms all that night. Las Vegas. Fast times, fast people. If Roxanne had wanted carefree fun, she couldn't have picked a better spot.

The last thing any of them expected was for Roxanne to walk into the apartment shortly after noon the next day, but she did. Frank ran to her instantly, enveloping her so fully in his arms that she was unaware of their audience. Corey and Corinne were excited to see her but remained in the background.

"I'm sorry, Frank," she wailed. "I'm so sorry—"

"No, I'm the one who's sorry. I didn't take the time to listen and hear—"

"I thought I'd go off... live it up to spite you, but I was only spiting myself... missed you and Jeffrey—"

"Thank God you're safe—"

"I went to Las Vegas—"

"I know. I had nightmares that you'd be picked up by some slick weasel—"

"You knew?"

"We hired an investigator—"

"We?"

Frank released his hold enough for her to look past him to the spot where Corinne was waiting.

"Cori?" she cried through her tears. "Oh, Cori!" Unwilling to let go of Frank, she drew him across the room so that she could hug Cori with her free arm. "I'm sorry. You came all the way up from Baltimore."

"I wasn't in Baltimore, but it wouldn't have mattered where I'd been, I would have come anyway. I should have come sooner."

"Thank you," Roxanne whispered brokenly. She held Corinne for a moment longer, then eased back. Her gaze shifted to Corey, returned to Corinne, then shifted back to the tall, auburn-haired man. "This has to be Corey," she said softly. Eyes brimming, she held her arm his way and wrapped it snugly around his neck when he gave her a hug. "Cori mentioned you to me. She was always so evasive that I knew you had to be someone special. She mentioned your hair, and for my sister to notice a man's hair... I'm sorry I've dragged you both here."

"Don't be silly," Corey chided, then teased, "Do you think I'd have missed a chance to get a look at you? Cori won't let me near her grandmother. Seems to think I'll traumatize her."

The look Roxanne gave him when she drew back was one of amusement, but it didn't linger. Within seconds she was back in her husband's arms, burying her face against his shirt, holding him tightly.

Corinne and Corey returned to Hilton Head late that afternoon. Under other circumstances they would have stayed and visited with Roxanne and Frank. But they knew that the two needed time alone, and time with Jeffrey.

Corinne needed time, too. With the intense fear she'd felt for Roxanne having eased, she needed to think about what had happened. She knew that Roxanne and Frank would have adjustments to make and prayed that they'd seek out professional help if the communication between them didn't improve. Corey had been right, though. Corinne had done all she could. The rest would be up to Roxanne and Frank.

Still, Corinne wanted to put what had happened into perspective. She thought about it often as she went about her work, pushing it from her mind only when she was with Corey, when he filled her senses to overflowing. She knew that she was going to have to make a decision on her own future before long; two more weeks on Hilton Head and she'd have all the questionnaires and personal interviews she needed, completed and ready for the coders. Other than a final trip to formally present the results of the survey, her work on the island would be done.

Those two weeks passed with alarming speed, and their end found Corinne no closer to making a decision than she'd been at the start. She'd been increasingly busy with work, and she hadn't wanted anything to intrude on the time she spent with Corey.

She wasn't prepared for the fact that he'd reached a decision of his own. They were at the airport, waiting for her plane to be called, when he broached it.

"I've been doing a lot of thinking," he said, taking her hand and concentrating deeply on her pinkie.

Corinne knew that something was wrong. For the past twenty-four hours she'd been so preoccupied with the dread of leaving that she hadn't guessed Corey had been thinking beyond that. Her heart began to pound. If he mentioned her coming down again before that next official visit, she'd be thrilled. Likewise, if he mentioned his coming to see her in Baltimore. If he was going to mention marriage, she wouldn't know what to say.

"I think," he stated slowly, "that you ought to stay in Baltimore for a while."

The pounding of her heart increased. "You'll be up to visit?"

"No. I won't visit. I want you to have time to yourself. You need to think about certain things."

The only certain thing that entered Corinne's mind just then was quickly on her tongue. "You *are* tired of me. I knew it would happen. You want a chance to spread your wings again—"

"No!" he barked, his green eyes piercing. "Totally wrong."

"But you don't want to see me—"

"I want to see you. Every day and every night. For the next who-knows-how-many years. I want to *marry* you Corinne, but you're not ready for that. You say you love me, but sometimes I'm not sure why you do or to what degree. Maybe when you can look at our relationship from a distance, you'll be able to figure out what you want."

"I think I want marriage...."

"Thinking you want it isn't good enough. You have to know it. You have to *feel* it. If you only think you want it, then it's wrong."

"But—"

"I won't be seeing anyone else here. I don't want to see anyone else. I don't want you to see anyone, either. But if you want to, if that's what it'll take to help you decide what's right for you, then so be it."

"I don't want—" She was suddenly competing with the loudspeaker overhead.

"That's your plane." Clasping her hand tightly, he stood and brought her up beside him. "I'll say goodbye now. I don't think I can bear dragging this out." He kissed her softly, lingeringly. "I love you," he whispered against her mouth.

"Corey—"

He pressed a finger to her lips. "You know the rules." With a final kiss on her forehead, he turned and walked quickly away. He didn't look back to see the stricken expression on her face. He was long gone from sight before she lowered her head, and this time she was the one who made it onto the plane with mere seconds to spare before the door was sealed.

The trip was an agonizing one for Corinne. By the time she arrived back in Baltimore, she'd lived through a lifetime of emotions. Sorrow, loss, dejection, fear, despair—she knew each in its turn. What emerged as the force dominating her actions when she landed, though, was anger. Pure, unadulterated anger.

It was four o'clock in the afternoon. The first thing she did, suitcases and all, was to taxi to the office, where she gave an astonished Alan her notice. Then she taxied home, where she informed her grandmother that she'd be leaving the city. Without so much as opening her bags, she thrust them into a taxi and headed for the airport, where she managed to catch a late flight to Atlanta. Unfortunately, there was no flight that night into Savannah. She debated driving, but worried that, given her state of mind, she'd crash into the nearest guardrail. So she took a motel room near the airport for the night, most of which she spent pacing the floor in a stewing rage. That rage was positively flying by the time she'd connected with Savannah the next morning and taken a cab directly to Corey's office.

Dumping her bags inside the door, she stalked past the receptionist and stormed straight into Corey's office, slamming the door behind her with hurricane force. He'd barely looked up in shock when she let loose.

"How *dare* you do that to me!" Her hands were planted on her hips, her eyes were wide and seething, and she was shaking with anger, but nothing could have blunted her tirade. "Sending me away like that was the lowest, most despicable thing you've ever done! When you tell a woman you love her, you do *not* send her away. When she says that she loves you, you do *not* question her motives. When you say you want to marry her, you *don't* prove it by sending her into exile. Who in the hell do you think you are ordering me around like that? I have feelings, too, and I don't like them put through the wringer!"

His jaw had dropped open. Perhaps she thought he was about to speak, because she rushed on.

"And *don't* tell me about the rules, because you can take your Cardinal Rules and...and *shove* them. I can be every bit as bossy as you, Corey Haraden, and I say that we're getting married. I am *not* going back to Baltimore until we are, and then you'll come back with me to help me pack up my things. Is that clear?"

Corey had shut his mouth. Calmly, he leaned back in his chair. "You're looking a little disheveled, Corinne."

"Well, you're not looking so hot yourself," she retorted. "Your hair looks like you combed it with your fingers, you have bags under your eyes, your tie is knotted backward—"

"So I didn't sleep any better last night than you did," he said in that same, maddeningly placid voice.

"It's all your fault! If you'd talked to me, if you'd told me that you'd run out of patience, if you'd said that you didn't know what else to do... But to take such drastic measures? Corey, that was *inexcusable*!"

"So it was."

"And you're just going to sit there grinning? What kind of message do you think *that* gives me? Where's the man who's so impulsive and persistent? Hasn't anything I've said made the *slightest* impression on you?"

"Oh, yes."

She raised a finger. "I know. You stapled your pants to the chair."

"If that were the case," he said, rising slowly, "I'd simply step out of them." He was rounding the desk, reaching for her arm. It was obvious that he wasn't looking for a hug when he started walking with her in tow.

"What are you doing?"

"Taking you home."

She dug in her heels. "I am not going back to Baltimore." She was forced to stumble into step beside him when he continued toward the door.

"I'm taking you *home*. That's *my* home. *Our* home."

"Oh." She was practically trotting to keep up with him. "Does that mean you apologize?"

"Yup."

"We're getting married?"

"Yup."

They swept past the receptionist, then Corinne's bags. "Corey, my things..."

"Later."

"Aren't you going to say something more—like you love me, or you were worried sick, or you're glad to have me back?"

He turned to her as they waited for the elevator. "I love you. I was worried sick. I'm glad to have you back."

The elevator doors slid open. "You sound about as sincere as—" She grunted when he yanked her forward, but that was all she had time for. The doors weren't quite closed when he flattened her against the wall and covered her mouth with a kiss. It started with force, softened into persuasion, deepened with eloquently spoken love.

The elevator reached the ground floor. Its doors slid open. After a minute the doors slid closed, and it began to rise again.

On the ninth floor a group of businessmen got on. If one of them hadn't had the good sense to loudly clear his throat when they'd reached the ground again, Corey and Corinne might have made the trip several times more.

Corinne stirred against Corey. They were lying in the middle of the living room carpet, clothes strewed randomly about. They'd never made it to the bedroom.

She kissed the soft spot at the front of his armpit and slid her leg between his when his arm urged her closer.

"What did it, sweetheart?" he asked softly.

Her own voice was wispy, drowsy in the aftermath of the most fiery lovemaking she'd ever known. "I don't know. Maybe Roxanne. She had her chance but she didn't take it. If she'd been like Mother she'd never have returned. I mean, she's like Mother in some ways, but I realized that in other ways she's...herself. So I figured that the same might be true of me. Just because I love making love with you, it doesn't mean that I'm an indiscriminate nymphomaniac."

Corey chuckled.

"Then again," Corinne went on, twirling his chest hair around her finger, "maybe it was you. You've been too nice, too patient. Sending me away like that was an abrupt turnaround. It did to me what Rox's disappearance did to Frank. You were right, Corey. I was afraid to take a risk. Then I realized that the real risk would be trying to live without you." She kissed that same soft spot, aware that she could spend the rest of her life with Corey and never tire of that spot and others. "When I realized that I could easily lose you, I nearly went nuts."

"Nuts? Corinne Fremont going nuts?"

"Not a very rational reaction, I know. But that's how it was. So strong, so definitive that I knew. I *knew*." She felt his mouth against her hair and snuggled closer. "Corey?"

He'd never felt as content in his life. It was a struggle to produce any sound at all. "Hmm?"

"Did you plan it that way?"

"What?"

"When you sent me away, did you do it as a shock treatment?"

"I should be so clever."

"You didn't expect me back so soon?"

"Nope."

"I surprised you?"

"Yup."

"Pleasantly?"

"Ecstatically."

"What was that noise?"

"My stomach. I'm hungry."

She raised her head to look at him. "Didn't you have breakfast?"

"I tried. You know I'm not much good on my own in the morning."

She turned her head toward the hall, then sniffed. "What is that smell?"

"I told you I'm not much good on my own. I was missing you, which made it even worse."

"What *is* it?"

"English muffins. Scorched. I put them under the broiler, then got to thinking about you and forgot about them."

"I'm surprised Jontelle didn't air out—" She bolted up, eyes wide and on the door. Hugging her arms to her breasts, she whispered hoarsely, "Jontelle! Where *is* she?"

Corey laughed as he hoisted himself to his feet. "She called in sick this morning."

Corinne's eyes narrowed. "That was convenient. Are you *sure* you didn't know I was coming back?"

He gave her a hand up, then swept her all the way into his arms and strode off toward the kitchen. "If I'd known you were coming back, I wouldn't have been such a basket case. I wouldn't have left the bed in shambles—"

"Oh, no."

"Or wet towels all over the bathroom floor."

"You didn't."

"I had to. The floor was a mess."

"Why?"

"I picked up the shampoo to take it into the shower, only I'd forgotten to screw on the top the last time I used it. I was preoccupied, and before I knew what was happening, the whole thing had dropped and spilled all over—"

She groaned against his neck.

"—and I didn't want Jontelle to slip in the goo and fall, because I knew she was going to be furious enough with what I'd done to the oven."

"You mean...you did something...over and above incinerating the muffins?"

His voice grew gruff. "I said I was missing you. I wasn't thinking."

"What beyond the muffins?"

"Well, hell, how was I to know that you can't cook eggs in an oven?"

"You can, I suppose."

"Not in the shell. Eggs in shells explode. See, you didn't even know that, so it wasn't just a lovesick stupidity on my part. Anyway, it wouldn't have been all that bad if I hadn't tried to clean it up, real quick, while the oven was hot. The only problem was that I was so frustrated with the whole situation that I grabbed the wrong can. Let me tell you what roach killer does to carbonized egg yolks...."

# Take 3 of
## "The Best of the Best™" Novels FREE
## Plus get a FREE surprise gift!

National Bestselling Author

# JoAnn Ross

*Really steams it up this August with*

Jonnie Ryan had always loved Dan Kincade, the local
college basketball coach. Ever since the day when he'd
gently resisted her teenage longings, Jonnie knew that he
was something special. Now, years later, he was being
accused of shady campus sports practices and she just
couldn't stand by and watch his career and reputation being
destroyed. Jonnie was willing to risk her career to defend
Dan from the malicious accusations—but was she also
willing to admit that she'd never stopped loving him? And
would Dan finally see her as a woman and not a little girl?

Available wherever books are sold.

If you're looking for more titles by

**BARBARA DELINSKY**

Don't miss these passionate stories by one of
MIRA's most celebrated authors:

**MIRA**